1F THERE BE G1ANTS

THE WATCHERS † BOOK ONE

ELLISON BLACKBURN

goldbrier

Printed in the United States of America
10 9 8 7 6 5 4 3 2 1

ISBN: 978-0-9962300-9-4 (paperback)
ISBN: 978-0-9962300-6-3 (e-book)

Contents

Epigraph 1

Principles of Garbage 3
Divides That Bind.. 9
Everyday Carry 13
A Man About a Rock 17
Buried Treasure 23
Rough Drafting 27
Yay or Nay 31
Half in Clay...43
John Doe 49
Earth Quaking...55
Well, Golly..63
Everything's a Sell...69
Spiritual Matters..73
Drove Incoming 83
Glimpse of Trouble..89
The Grey Line 97
By Jove... 109
Crossed Paths 117
Man Friends.. 125
Containment 129
Multiplicity 139
To Each Their Own 149
Maybe Conscious 155
Graceless Girl 159
Grey Skies.. 171
Three Words 177
Felled No More 183
Safe and Unsound 191
Interrupted.. 197
Black Thoughts 203

Contents

The Giant Race.. 209

Unmarked Grey 217

Unreasonable Voices 219

Just a Dream.. 223

Accidentally Dying... 229

Fireflies 233

Homecoming.. 239

Story Time 243

Collective Brawn 251

A Weakened State 257

Life Is for the Living 263

The Ending 269

About the Author... 273

Titles by Ellison Blackburn.. 275

Epigraph

Passage

Breakable mannequin of clay,
 Who in life unwittingly trusts,
 But in death must,
 Traverse either veil.
What has he?
 But a sliver of time,
 To decide his prime,
 In a reality made unreal.
The choice is his,
 For the soul only guides,
 As the mind overrides,
 Once even weights upon the scale.
Shed off this earthly coil,
 A garment of dove or crow,
 Beyond the colorless glow,
 For desires are emptied when he dies.

Principles of Garbage

†

D R. MALLORY JACKS had spent thirty odd years of her life studying garbage, literally. The basic principle of archaeology has always been one person's trash is a ditch digger's treasure. Or something to that effect. Buried among what would seem inconsequential bits of pottery, fragments of bone from former meals and the death of animals, and other cast offs of bygone civilizations were the many invisible intrigues. For Mallory, there was a certain comfort in uncovering the stories of those who once lived. She enjoyed unraveling those tales, a minuscule and sometimes not so tiny, puzzling piece at a time.

She grew up watching one Indiana Jones adventure after another and then in repetition. Immersing herself in the qualifications of two of her idols, she began carrying around a novice kit, so as to be never in a predicament where she found herself without at least the essentials. Weapons of the trade and ammunition or "everyday carry" as her father, a former military man, called it. Of course, instead of the aggressive pistols, daggers, and swords used to kill people past and present, an anthropologist's armaments were wielded with a feather light touch, hoping to revive the ghosts of the long dead.

The then nine-year-old aspirant stocked her father's small, old army backpack with the following: a magnifying glass for close inspection of the area without disturbing the scene; a sheet of waxed paper and a small piece of linen, both folded neatly inside a metal cigarette case to be used either as clean surfaces on which she could study her find or to wrap it with care for later scrutiny; a two-inch, flat, soft-bristle paint brush for dusting the surroundings as well as another, finer one for cleaning debris off from the found object; several rubber bands for whatever purpose (endlessly useful tools); an empty, leak-proof soap dish for rinsing and storing findings; and a canteen always filled with fresh water, again for various reasons.

Even as an adolescent, Mallory was not shy; on the contrary, if one knew her. To everyone else, she appeared to be a quiet and reserved child, tending to shirk offers of friendship from just *any*body. In fact, she was driven toward adventures of the solitary kind, preferring the company of her surroundings over playing make believe among fantasies she was not interested in and were not of her own making. As a result, her classmates called her names, such as "Manly" for her tomboy ways or "Lonely Jacks." She did not find the insults offending because she simply didn't care.

Thus, for several years, every day after school she would throw off her school bag, exchange it for her kit, and skip off on her own personal archaeological dig. Her neighborhood had been expanding during that time, but around the Jacks residence on the outskirts of Tucson, there was also always a vacant field—be it a construction site or yet undeveloped land—ready for her exploration.

When she and her family moved to England, it wasn't lost friendships she mourned. As mentioned, she wasn't the *attaching* type and as children do, she adjusted to both the new landscape and weather of Cornwall in a matter of weeks. In fact, the town of Ivers was better than Tucson for a budding earth-and-dead-people detective, she decided. The artifacts she uncovered in the foreign soil were mysterious; completely unlike anything she'd found before.

Surprisingly, not long after their relocation, Mallory made a friend too, just the way she liked to make friends—without trying. Paisley, unlike her new and strange boon companion, wasn't as socially inept, yet she was as strong willed and keen as Mallory. By the time Mallory turned thirteen, a mere six months later, although her knowledge was gleaned from obsessive research—and one credible source, her mother, a British native—more so than by self-discovery, she was spouting facts about buried treasures to anyone who would listen. That audience was still mainly her mom and dad, but now Paisley as well, a possible convert and fellow apprentice.

To don the persona more completely for her friend's sake, or so she said, Mallory began prefacing her backyard findings with "Trust me, kid. This tin has a story to tell," refined from its earlier version, "Uh, trust me, kid. This tin can has a story to tell …" Yet, at thirteen and a half, she decided she needed a shtick of her own. She sampled, "We have indeed found a storytelling treasure," "Ah! An interesting find, my dear Watson. We must uncover its story," and "Hm, most intriguing, to be sure." Finally, she chose: "Mark me, kid. A telltale piece is what we have here." She was not about to abandon her favorite part of Indy's original phrase (since she absolutely worshiped the fact that to him everyone was a kid).

She eventually went back to her old saying. It rolled off the tongue easier and she wasn't modeling Sherlock Holmes, after all. Nor was she practicing to become a stuffy academic. Albeit a professor, Indiana Jones was definitely not stuffy. He certainly would not have phrased his statements and curiosity so haughtily. Although she didn't know it, Mallory's sense of identity was still a confused work-in-progress. Her upbringing through to adolescence was pinned to her American roots, and her impressionable teenage brain was still being bombarded with truths of an entirely different environment and culture.

Like other schoolmates, Paisley Bourne initially thought her friend just strangely American and perhaps a little uncouth. Her parents ill-judged Mallory as well. However, although prudishly at first, after joining in on more than one adventure, Paisley discovered her own penchant for the subdued thrills of the dig. Soon she was contributing in her own way. For instance, she suggested the idea of adding a pickax, two sharpened pencils, and a steno pad to their kits. In addition, rather than saying anything to pronounce her discoveries, she took to pointing vaguely at the ground, then tapping the side of her nose, raising one eyebrow, and lowering the other. Without having to ask, Mallory interpreted Paisley's gesture to mean, "Something is fishy," and that was usually the case.

Together these industrious youths scoured the hillsides and cliffs of Ivers for fossils, bones, and mysterious parts and pieces of objects. Soon enough, bookshelves were littered with crinoid stems. Windowsills were covered in broken glassware and crockery. Mobiles were constructed of pieces of metal and plastic as well as candy wrappers and then hoisted aloft from the rafters with fishing wire.

Over a short time, much to Mr. And Mrs. Bourne's dismay, Paisley's bedroom too was transformed into what they dubbed "rubbish style." Mr. and Mrs. Jacks were accustomed to the mess in Mallory's room, but in the Bourne household, it progressively became a point of parental contention and conversely, teenage angst. Unless Paisley could somehow demonstrate the purpose of the accumulating junk, the contents of her room were at risk of ending up in a garbage can.

Brilliantly, Paisley managed to elevate the tiniest fragment to "relic" status by cleaning each piece and cataloging it meticulously in her notebook. She was then in a position to effectively negotiate a truce with her parents on the basis of the inventory. The reframing of the finds as worthy artifacts—pieces she and Mallory would have agreed were really trash—was another reason Mallory believed her and Paisley were together a well-balanced, whole adult (while each still being a developing person).

Divides That Bind

†

T HESE YEARS OF youth flew by and soon college as well as the world of professional experience parted the two friends for nearly a decade. However lengthy, both still knew the separation was temporary. At the onset, they'd agreed that the vast distance of many thousands of miles—as Paisley attended university in the United States and got her first big break working for the Smithsonian National Museum of Natural History in Washington D. C.—would not drive a wedge in their sisterhood. Frequently, almost daily, she and Mallory talked or sent messages to one another.

By July of 2007, anthropologist, Dr. Mallory Jacks returned to Ivers from Edinburgh, Scotland. Dr. Paisley Bourne, museum curator arrived a month later. Although they'd coordinated the homecoming, what course their lives would take professionally, after the fact, was approached differently by each.

For Mallory, life would be more of an ongoing adventure led by uncertainty; in other words, she would improvise. As was customary for her line of work, she'd just go where the artifacts were to be found. Fortunately, she now knew people or *connections* to tell her where to be and when. Not exactly serendipitously, one of those persons was her best friend, but simply put, Ivers would be Mallory's home base and the rest of

Great Britain her remote office.

On the other hand, Paisley made plans for the future based decidedly on professional ambitions. Being a trained museum administrator, she decided Ivers needed a menagerie of sorts of its own. Creating one was to be her second, or rather, third calling. From the tiniest details, Paisley Bourne, entrepreneur, systematically set her notions into action. First, she carefully considered the name of the institution; too narrow might imply the findings were all local and would perhaps seem quaint. (Ivers was small, and if not sleepy, then oddly sedate.) Yet, too broad would connote the opposite.

That Paisley should ruminate over this seemingly minor detail for weeks was somewhat outside of Mallory's mental grasp, but she also knew Paisley had a rationale for everything. "A financial plan, including both the red and the black of it, is the crux of any solid business. If I cannot sell our cause or compete with established museums, Mallory, it'll be very hard to gain the funding grants we'll need to excavate anything more than what can be dug up with a pickaxe and a trowel," her partner explained.

Finally, Paisley settled on calling the rented, two-room building, the Lands End Museum of Man (LEMM), even though from day one through three hundred it was just a lofty name for the artifacts she and Mallory had gathered from their childhood adventures. The same fossils and litter that adorned the sills and shelves of their bedrooms were cleaned, labeled, and set on display behind sterile glass cases.

Next, according to standard establishment bylaws, the museum should have a board. Thus, Mallory became a member, although again, apart from making archaeological contributions and sitting in on meetings from time to time she didn't do much; running a business, non-profit or otherwise, wasn't her forte. Regardless, she and Paisley made a good team; they understood each other's limitations and strengths. For example, Paisley knew that in order for each of them to excel in her chosen profession and be happy with her efforts on that front, they both needed to remain somewhat independent of one another. Mallory did not *want* to be involved in the logistics of running a business, whereas that side of the arrangement, besides being very capable at it, is what Paisley found more to her own liking.

Mallory's father was inducted into a seat on the board as well since, according to Paisley, his experience as a history professor was relevant to LEMM's mission. Other members, two of Paisley's former professors as well as Everett Brandt, chairman of the British Isles Anthropological Institute (BIAI) were offsite, so to speak.

Slowly, somehow, Paisley managed to acquire some pieces on loan while LEMM's acquisition collection was being built. It was not until nine years later that the museum passed the provincial mark, filled then with interesting finds from all over the Isles. With display cabinets stocked, the placeholder artifacts were slowly once again restored to their original, non-sterile homes. Still, a substantial portion of the LEMM collection was Cornish, since many of Drs. Jacks's and Bourne's projects were sponsored by the museum and supporters of it.

Everyday Carry

†

THE SAME FADED and stained, canvas backpack she'd been toting around for nearly twenty-eight years was a prized possession. Mallory traced a light touch over the embroidered initial M. and Jacks. Her father, who she was named after, died two years ago last week—not that she needed the bag as a reminder of the still grief-inducing fact.

"Go see what you can dig up, Junior." She smiled to herself, hearing the humorous lilt of Mallory senior's voice in her head. An analyst of highbrow historical texts and lover of erudite poetry, he had loved the simplicity of a good pun.

Whenever he'd called her "Junior" she would offer an exaggerated salute as she clicked her heels together, and rebutted, "Yes, S-er *Senior* Citizen," although, he wasn't quite that old.

He'd laugh every time and maybe even jokingly reprimand her afterward. Recalling one such lecture, she stared at the name sadly *and proudly*.

"The initial there, M, is conveniently versatile as it can also stand for *Major* Jacks of the 1968 United States Intelligence Corps, and so, '*Sir*' is right! Remember, I'm not so much in *your* service as *you are* in mine, *junior* officer of the Jacks household. I am *your* senior, after all." He'd added in a shielded whisper, "Only your mother ranks higher than me in these, our barracks, Corporal Jacks … but don't tell her I acknowledge it. Come to think of it, I shall have to start calling you Junior Peon if we're to maintain protocol."

Mallory's mother, Angel, as she was called among her circle of friends and by Mr. Jacks, died as well in the same car crash; she was only fifty-five years old. Anjali Jacks was a mathematics schoolteacher, a woman of impeccable character, a habitual teetotaler, and actually, a black tea addict. Her pretty face would scrunch up with guilt when all she could offer a guest was Earl Grey or Orange Pekoe; as she herself had an affinity with Darjeeling and found it unfathomable others would not have indicated their preference for the same had they a choice.

"Ay! Senior Peon, chop chop. I need those veggies diced nice and small, that is, sometime before your shift is over and we all die from starvation," responded her mother, whisking her hand over the produce. She smiled innocently and nibbled the outer edge of a slice of cucumber for effect.

Mallory thought the way her mother moved was as if poetry were embodied. She didn't for a moment imagine she was as graceful.

When her father dallied longer, with her back turned toward the stove, Mrs. Jacks had said, "That is a command, Major, darling." Mallory also loved the way her mom made that soft purring sound when speaking words containing the letter R.

Opening the flap of the backpack, she scanned the contents before securing the metal clasps closed and hoisting it over one shoulder. Quickly texting as she walked toward the door, she notified Paisley where they'd meet and to be ready in five minutes for pickup.

A Man About a Rock

†

MGs WERE NOT necessarily trustworthy vehicles, but Mallory's old car was an exception and an hour later, they'd arrived. She disengaged the clutch, shifted the car into neutral, and pulled the key abruptly out of the ignition. The car crunched up the slightly sloped gravel drive a few dozen feet before finally sputtering to a halt. She yanked the parking brake with force when the motor wheezed its final breaths of death. Beside her, Paisley snickered.

"Sometimes I think this contraption creepy; Christine's poor, English relation." She pet the dashboard tentatively and then jiggled the door handle again. Undoing the seatbelt, she shoved awkwardly at the door.

"You know she likes a little tough love, put some muscle into it," Mallory instructed. Through the windshield window, she ducked and scanned the whitewashed exterior of the farmhouse looming in front of them. "It's quite nice having friends on top or should I say, in low—"

"A teensy bit off-colour that was," Paisley replied, twisting her lips, half smiling, half in mock disgust.

"What?" Mallory asked somewhat absently, turning toward Paisley but glancing to either side past her head.

"Keaton. You were saying being his friend has *certain*

17

benefits. Hmm?" She tried to maneuver around in the narrow bucket seat to catch a glimpse of the scene behind her.

"Your brother is … well, I always get my news hot off the presses, or before it even makes it there, is what I meant." The surrounding fields were empty, except for a lone figure off to the distance. "That must be Mr. Fritchey over there." Mallory pointed over Paisley's shoulder. "Not that I'm complaining, but why did Keaton call me before you?" she asked, distracted by the man holding a shovel aloft as if he were going to strike something.

Again, Paisley attempted a peek. The space inside the cab was too cramped for her to look in the direction Mallory gestured. She'd meet their host soon enough. The sight they'd come to see wasn't going anywhere either. "Maybe I missed his call. Even if he called you first, you should know why by now. An excuse … my daft brother has had a crush on you from day one. No, wait." She paused briefly. "I can actually pinpoint the day when his barminess began. You were fourteen years old, and as per usual, wearing the look of a vagabond rather well."

"Mm." Mallory murmured, rummaging in her bag. She had written the farmer's full name, along with details of the land in her notebook.

"You'd stomped into my house just as I was setting the table for supper. Outraged by your lack of success a third or fourth day in a row, you didn't notice my mum enter the room. It was quite funny, really. My proper, English house and you obliviously American, standing there sullying my mum's carpets with mud and her ears with, 'Blast! And double blast! Not so much as a coin or a condom wrapper for my trouble.'

Remember? Mum started re-questioning whether you were a good influence on me." Paisley chuckled and Mallory bobbed her head, grinning as she pulled out a few articles from the backpack. "You made a different impression on Keaton," Paisley continued. "Frozen on the stair landing, he stared down at you like a dog having spotted a previously hidden but guarded bone. Stupidly grinning and blushing, he looked as though he wanted to lick you clean."

"Not sure your brother would appreciate that likeness, and I don't remember the scene as vividly but Keaton sounds like the pedophile he was."

"Aly, questionable though his tastes may have been—you have to admit, you were a mangy creature back then—a sixteen-year-old boy's crush is hardly illegal. He was just being completely normally hormonal."

"Say that three times fast."

"Regardless of how he felt, you've been like a sister to both of us. Anyway, why don't you two stop the farce? Just snog and be done with it."

"Now *that* was rather indelicate, Paiz," Mallory smirked.

"Why? You're no prude."

"Suggesting I carry on with my supposed ... besides, for your information, the day he left for uni he semi-officially became an offender."

"What do you mean?"

"Three days after turning eighteen, consensual or not, he assaulted a minor. Let's just say, there was ... ehm, groping involved and the kisses were *not* ones a brother gives his sister. Good thing I've always thought him just *your* brother."

Paisley shot Mallory a wide eyed, electric glance; obviously, she was not aware of that farewell meeting.

However, incognizant of the special interest her friend was taking in these childhood escapades and the fact that they were for some reason still sitting in the car, Mallory revealed her notepad and flipped to the last page. Perusing her scribblings, she announced, "Daniel. His name is Daniel Fritchey. The land has been used as a livestock farm for several generations, mostly sheep and dairy cattle it seems. The Fritcheys own about fifty acres. Slight irrigation gradation to the west and—"

"Well, do it again. Over a couple of decades ago hardly counts." Paisley interrupted. "First comes love, then comes marriage, and voila its baby Kelly in a baby carriage. La la la." She eyed the door and halfheartedly jiggled the handle for the third time. She was trying to be nonchalant about Mallory and her brother's excruciatingly slow-budding romance, but secretly nothing would make her happier than seeing her two favorite people together.

"I'll propose this evening. It'll be a very civil ceremony followed by wedded bliss by the end of the week. Give us a minute for Kelly, eh? We'll place the order for that parcel as soon as possible." Without waiting for a reply, in one swift move Mallory opened the door and slid out of the car.

"Sounds good," mumbled Paisley, smiling thinly. Finally, shouldering the door she gave it a nice, forceful shove. It opened with a protesting groan. Climbing out, the relief was so great she too sighed as she stretched her long limbs. She was tall—of Amazonian proportions—at five feet, ten inches barefooted, with the broad shoulders, and the muscular frame to match. The Bournes bore a striking resemblance to one another, in both features and physique. The family of four was good looking in a superhero sort of way; they all had jet-black hair, ice-blue eyes, and very fair complexions. Keaton was six feet tall, if not a smidgeon taller and by far the most unreal in his perfect features.

The Jacks's, on the other hand, were averagely built, none of them over five feet nine inches tall. Still, Mr. Jacks had been debonair in appearance and stature. Even late in his fifties, he looked thirty something; handsome, lean, and fit, having kept his military bearing over the years. He was fair complexioned and blonde with green eyes. Mrs. Jacks was petite and curvaceous; exotically pretty with long, lustrous, near-black locks; chocolate colored eyes; and naturally burgundy lips amidst a heart-shaped, light-brown face. Upon very close inspection, looking past her more muted coloring, in features, Mallory took slightly more after her mother than father. She wore her multi-faceted, mid to light brown and gold, straight hair in a comfortable chin-length style, having abandoned the need for tiebacks. Her wide, almond shaped, hazel eyes were fringed with dark, thick lashes; and her soft pink lips were not as wide or full as her mother's, nor were they as thin as her father's, although his could not really have been called thin.

Neither Paisley nor Mallory, based solely upon appearance had difficulty finding short-term companions who could fulfill physical desires or provide the tiny bit of emotional affirmation that usually comes with shallow romantic relationships. The operative word, *short-term* was modus operandi for the friends.

Although it was for reasons of her own that each woman had chosen singlehood as a way of life thus far and maybe even for the remaining part of it. Perhaps, Mr. Jacks was too hard of an act to follow and that was why Mallory and Keaton were not together, theirs could not be a fling.

Buried Treasure

†

ARLY ON THE morning of April 11, Daniel Fritchey contacted the regional press, specifically, The Endish Daily. It was Keaton Bourne who happened to take that call. By the time Drs. Mallory Jacks and Paisley Bourne reached the site at eleven o'clock, the ground had been already trampled with a hundred muddy footprints. Thankfully, the gawkers had remained outside of the haphazard hole Mr. Fritchey had dug. Fortuitously, by now everyone else had lost interest it seemed.

In the ditch was the single stone of a henge—like numerous others across the country—both an uncommon and banal sight for the residents of the British Isles. It was almost a rule for every community to have one, some had a complete circle, others two structures. Certainly, the town of Gwellen must have felt somewhat inadequate up until now.

Mr. Fritchey had obligingly washed the visible part of the stone and the anthropologists sauntered around the site in assessment. Paisley jotted down a bulleted list in an ordinary spiral bound notepad while Mallory scrutinized the scene, taking mental notes. At a glance, beyond the dirty streaks from the washing, there were several white scuffs on the stone where the farmer's shovel had scratched its surface. For thousands of years the granite had remained unblemished, undamaged; yet, one brief encounter with a man and its easterly face was marred with scars—forevermore. A small chip exposed an inner layer of the stone of a lighter gray color, but this wasn't a detail the inquisitors needed to know. In fact, it was something the experts would have preferred *not* knowing.

Paisley shook her head and grimaced as she scribbled. Mallory grinned to herself; she knew what her partner wanted to say to the ignoramus who'd done the vandalizing, but unfortunately, this kind of thing happened all too often. Discoveries were regularly made by accident and the accidents themselves were frequently damaging. Judging by the accomplice shovel wedged into the un-dug ground, adjacent to one end of the ditch and next to a murky bucket of water with a filthy rag draped over its rim, Mallory was only glad the aged farmer had stopped his enthusiastic investigation. It looked as though he'd had a good go of it before losing his gumption, however.

For all Mr. Fritchey's effort, only a small portion of the stone was exposed. This much was obvious. However, *small*, relative to a typical henge stone was actually a lot, at least, when compared to excavations of other burial sites. This was what Dr. Jacks surmised in her professional capacity hengiform were, in part, tombstones; not for giants, but rather, collectively, they were markers for an ancient community—a single monument encompassing many peoples and serving multiple purposes.

Modern imagination would lead a person to think of a gravestone as a small, sometimes precision cut, slab of concrete, embedded over a grave with possibly a brief inscription for whom it was made to tribute. However, henge were hewn thousands of years ago; precision was limited by the hand eye coordination of a human machine, the craftsman, as well as the available crude tools at his disposal. Some stones were jagged and rough, others smooth and almost polished. Tombstones or not, contemporary or ancient, all were crafted without any identification. Today, there was still no way to tell the difference without an often complex analysis of the environment.

One or two stone circles known to historians contained a single crude stone pallet or boulder in the center. This lone, often smaller structure was accepted among the professional community as perhaps a grave marker for an esteemed leader. However, Dr. Jacks's opinion differed somewhat from that of her other colleagues in the field. Most anthropologists would argue the main purpose of a circle was as a congregation place for pagan rituals, an open-air church of sorts. While she accepted this as one and possibly the primary use, Mallory was also well aware that most later churches included graveyards. She postulated that the pagans might have practiced rites *among* their deceased. From what she understood of those peoples, she didn't believe it likely they would have excluded their departed loved ones from the sacred grounds within the circle; thus, making the entirety of a hengiform a cemetery as well. The main problem with her theory lay with the archaeology. Very few biological remains, other than that of sacrificial animals, had been found at excavation sites. Add to that the statistical improbability of a henge being unearthed; it wasn't done often.

Hengiform typically protruded, making what existed beneath the surface the greater mystery; the footage above was sometimes reflected below. Although the Easter Island stones in the Galapagos were not henge stones by the traditional definition, they were prime examples of facets of antique structures that could remain hidden for centuries or forever. It was just recently discovered that these guardians bore immense full, subsurface bodies to go along with their colossal, exposed heads. Thus, the fact that the Gwellen boulder was buried completely underground made it slightly unique and by a cursory but knowledge driven assumption, older than your normal henge—if any antiquity could be considered ordinary.

Rough Drafting

†

THE RAIN PERSISTED in its slow and steady English way. The two-foot wide and equally deep ditch was now partially filled with mustard colored water. The gully outlined roughly a fourth of the stone's perimeter, which Mallory estimated would then be twenty-four feet all the way around. From the visible surface area, it looked as though Mr. Fritchey's henge stone was somewhere in between an enormous rock found and placed on the spot, as is, and one that had been sculpted smooth. Moving the stone itself would have taken great effort but the doctors couldn't tell yet how much care was taken in its actual construction.

Paisley tucked away her notebook and pencil in the large patch pocket of her mackintosh and stepped away to speak with Mr. Fritchey (forewarning him of the logistical next steps). Mallory watched the farmer nod tersely and numerously as she messaged the foreman of her usual dig crew. She then rang up the permits office to submit a formal application for the excavation. It shouldn't take more than a day or two for the necessary clearance, especially since both Drs. Jacks and Bourne were well known throughout the area for having uncovered other historically significant pieces, such as Dundien, the small but very old funeral pyre, just twenty miles southeast of the tiny borough of Gawain in the Bodmin Moor.

The existence of a notable institution, such as LEMM, also brought acclaim to Ivers and thereby the region.

Gwellen was luckily a small community. From here on out, there might be the stray passerby or the odd visitor, but the area would be easily quarantined so curious individuals could not come too near the artifacts. Therefore, the ground would no further be disturbed by inexperienced traffic. In Mallory's mind, there was little doubt that this was not the only gargantuan stone in Mr. Fritchey's field; such stones were rarely standalone bodies.

An hour later, Mallory deposited her stiff-legged friend in front of LEMM and she herself went back to the house—her parent's house—to outline the specifications of the scene and write up a concise description. Every project was a case study. However, as her concentration was the anthropology of the civilizations that utilized stone circles, much of this first report would be a repeat of earlier projects. The goal was always to find something new in order to build upon current knowledge.

Next was a rough draft of the timeline, taking into consideration the very few known facts at this juncture, such as soil conditions and natural landmarks. There were also no nearby man-made mounds or trenches on Mr. Fritchey's land. These facts alone would seem to make this a straightforward study. The last henge project the doctors were involved with took a couple of months, but the stones were above ground. The work was done mostly with special equipment, such as deep level foreign matter detectors and sonic cameras. Protocol for such finds was more restrictive since local governments were less likely to grant dig permissions when the artifacts in question were already visible, albeit partially. This also meant, these types of enterprises were completed faster.

One glaring aforementioned difference made the Gwellen site unique from any other study of the kind. That variable implied a much longer road ahead for this particular project—also making it imperative it be approached hands on. To reiterate, the Gwellen henge was buried.

Taking this special situation into consideration, Mallory began to make a list of people resources and equipment for the actual excavation. Once the permits were attained, it would take roughly a week just to identify and mark the area and for the overburden of topsoil to be removed. After that, a few student recruits from the university's anthropology department would need to be requested. Mallory would be tasked with the role of their monitor and overall excavation manager since Paisley would oversee the finds, the budget, and everything else from the administration side. The silent partner—*money*—with whom Paisley held a close relationship, said students were the most economical option and only their *free* hands would make other requirements possible.

Mallory grazed her bottom lip back and forth with the end of the pen and then bit down on the cap. There was one doctoral candidate she had worked with in the past who showed promise at the time and was helpful without being too needy. Underlining his name, she hoped to retain Grey McKnight and a few other graduate students. Underclassmen would be fine too, but from her experience, she knew the archaeologist wannabes would be naively disrespectful of the site and artifacts. They would require a higher level of babysitting.

Yay or Nay

†

"GREY OUT," MALLORY said obliquely and pointed toward the ladder. Her favorite student nodded and left immediately, although he had been working diligently on another part of the grid entirely. He usually grinned crookedly when she issued abrupt commands; however, he also never questioned her authority.

Quickly she threw a tarp over the artifact in the two-meter square she'd been working, pinning the corners down with metal stakes through the grommet holes and tapping each stake with a hand shovel to secure it into the tough ground. She stood there for a second, staring at the grayish-taupe colored plastic in awe, as though the covering was transparent. Then, hustling out of the pit, and once she reached ground level, she dusted her hands on the thighs of her khakis. Still dazed, when she looked up, she noticed the student members of the dig team peering over the edge of the pit.

Splaying her arms on either side, she stalked forward, ushering them away and saying brusquely, "Back up. Everyone get you a cup of bad coffee and a nice comfortable, if rickety, seat in the tent. Dr. Bourne and I will meet you there in thirty minutes." The group hesitated and one student continued to gape into the depths of the pit, from which now nothing could be revealed. "Ambrose, I mean it. If you can't follow simple instructions, you're out." She raised her eyebrows questioningly at Grey. "That goes for all of you."

Again, Grey smirked, but immediately turned and stalked away toward the meeting tent.

Contained though it was, Mallory's state of panic and excitement brimmed beneath the surface of her facade. In search of Paisley, she jogged in the opposite direction as the others had gone. Paisley would most likely be found in the smaller of the two structures that were erected on the site—the artifacts tent. Sure enough, her colleague sat there holding a pair of tweezers aloft, which pinched between its prongs held a tiny fragment of gold-colored metal. At the very moment, Mallory walked in the door. Rather than inspecting the relic in question, Dr. Bourne's head was bent over a ledger. With an old school, yellow, lead pencil, she scribbled the item's specifications into the catalog. She glanced up, opened her mouth to speak, paused mid-utter, and set the artifact down carefully inside a box lined with cotton batting. Shortly thereafter, they went down to the pit.

A half an hour later, "You are a breath away from being a part of something quite astounding," Paisley announced to the five students seated before them. She stood with her legs slightly spread apart and her arms folded across her chest. Her presence was commanding enough. Being told once or twice in her youth that she looked even more like Wonder Woman when she stood with her hands on her hips, she usually thereafter opted to take up this more defensive posture. Not that being likened to a superhero was a bad thing; it was just that with it came some kind of expectation. While she struck high on most of her goals, she preferred to think of them as *personal* ambitions. The truth was she didn't want to worry about not meeting the expectations of others and thus, facing their disappointment on any level if she failed.

"However, before we can tell you what this is all about, a few new rules need to be put in place that we before hadn't bothered with," Mallory stated matter-of-factly. Her arms lay stiffly on either side, palms flat and nearly touching her thighs.

"That is to say, rules were unnecessary as of yesterday,"— Paisley interjected and then hesitated, looking at Mallory— "since you are all aware of normal excavation processes, for the most part." Her partner nodded resolutely in agreement.

Pivoting on her ankles, holding up one finger so they all saw, Mallory began, "One, from here on out you cannot speak to anyone about this project, not your professors, not your girl or boyfriend, not your mum. If we so much as hear a peep around town, *all* of you will be off the project. Absolutely and immediately. And I do mean *all* since once the news gets out; we're not going to waste our time trying to figure out whom the leak was. Got that? If you cannot abide by this rule, then you're welcome to excuse yourself now." She and Paisley decided, although the students were needed, they would provide ample opportunities for anyone to leave.

Nigel coughed and then cleared his throat. "Eh-hem."

This was not the time for questions or discussion; opening the floor to one would inevitably shift the speeches away from the purpose of this gathering. Therefore, Mallory ignored the student's raised hand.

He tried again. "Dr. Ja—"

Eyeing him directly she said, "And … before we hear anything from you that borders on semantics, this goes for Ivers or any place reachable via phone, the internet, psychic connection. Some of you don't live around here; your homes may be in the vicinity of Lands End. So you know, it doesn't matter; we'll be watching the ever-sphere. We have spies everywhere."

"And if you choose to leave, you will still get your course credit, but won't be allowed on the site afterward. Just so that, as well, is made clear." Paisley added.

"Yes, but, Dr. Jacks, can you tell us a little more so we can decide if we want to be involved going forward?" Ambrose asked casually without preamble. "Is it really cool? Like uh … an uh … some Aztec treasure? Well, because so far it's only been rubbish."

At the remark from the undergraduate, the corners of Mallory's mouth quirked crookedly. "Are you serious? That's principle number one of anthropology. As scientists in this field, studying trash is what we do for the most part. I'm surprised it wasn't the first sentence in your textbook from ANTH 101. Did any of you sign up for this project knowing what you'd find five metres below ground level? Did visions of a cache of crystal skulls, King Tutankhamen's cousin's mummy, or a solid gold ark from the lost city of Atlantis dance in your head?—more examples that are highly unlikely. We're in Cornwall remember. Ambrose, first we'll sort the rules then, the piece de resistance will be revealed. So, you're either in or out. Although I do have to say, for some of you underclassmen, if you're *still* wondering if this is truly your calling, then I suggest you check off another day tossed into the great trash bin of life and make an appointment with an advisor tomorrow to change your concentration."

"Blimey. That's not very encouraging," Ambrose replied, smirking at Cara, who sat placidly beside him.

Mallory scoffed, repositioning a few stray strands of hair behind her ear on one side. "Mm, and speaking of advisors, it's not their job to discourage you from a career path. In that vein, it isn't for Dr. Bourne or myself to advise you either way, but I'll say this, we definitely would not encourage you. You see, a career in anthropology is much like getting an English Literature diploma. There isn't much you can do with it if you don't continue toward further schooling and in the end if academia is your goal, good luck! Only about six percent of *Harvard* graduates go on to become full on professors in either field."

"To append to Dr. Jack's earlier point, if you are under the assumption this is how every excavation will be then you're ninety-nine percent correct. Every dig will be like the last five weeks, resulting in nothing seemingly extraordinary while being done for a purpose. There will be levels of excitement, but you have to be able to find value in, as well as stay engrossed in, whatever you find, be it a chewing gum wrapper from ten years ago or the phalange of an Australopithecus afarensis. In most cases, you'll only have a vague idea of what you're looking for, in other words, a henge stone jutting out shan't be a sign. In fact, excavation of visible artefacts is prohibited."

"Uh finger of an Australian what-sit?" Ambrose pressed his lips together, at the same time raising his eyebrows crookedly. "Yeah, I think this is not for me. Can't see myself … what's the word? ... *bored* with my day job for the rest of my life. I don't even chew gum. I just *cannot* relate, so Sayonara peeps." He stood and looked around at his peers, possibly waiting for someone to try to stop him. "Cara, are you having fun yet? Or were you expecting to ... eventually? I admit, I sorta was, but that's shot."

The usually timid girl rose from her seat hastily, causing the folding chair to collapse and clatter to the floor in a heap behind her. Startled by the ruckus, she exclaimed, "Blast! What the—" Cara rolled her eyes toward the ceiling, her face coloring mildly. She slowly swiveled halfway to eye the offending chair. Turning back around, she shrugged and said, "Sorry, Dr. Jacks. Um, and, Dr. Bourne."

Mallory smiled kindly while thinking two disjointed thoughts, one after the other. That had taken longer than necessary and Cara exhibited more energy in those few seconds than either she or Paisley had witnessed in the past few weeks. "No worries at all. Grey, India, Nigel?"

"I'm staying," Grey responded unhesitatingly.

"Me, as well."

"Me, three."

"Ambrose, Cara, thank you both for your help thus far. Dr. Jacks will contact the school to make sure you get partial credit, and let them know your dismissal was not that, but rather a voluntary move on your part."

"Thanks. My mum'll be happy to know I'll be moving on from this 'financially grave career choice,' ... no offence, those were her words. Looks like it's medical school for me," Ambrose said. Mallory smiled and nodded and Dr. Bourne escorted the two undergraduate students out of the tent, watched them walk away, before returning to the others.

"All right folks, on with the rules." Mallory resumed, raising two fingers. "From this point forward, under no circumstances are you to go down to the pit without either Dr. Bourne or me. Three, you *will not* take it upon yourself to handle the artefact unless told to do so and are given specific instructions; we want no accidental damages made." She stepped aside to reveal equipment on the table behind her. "Four, each of you will be assigned one of these. It is your dedicated project device, in which you can enter all of your notes and a recap of what you've accomplished each day you are here. Absolutely no more paper notes are allowed. You will also check in your mobiles and check out your devices prior to beginning each shift and the reverse whenever you leave each day. If Dr. Bourne is not in the tent at either time, you'll just have to find her."

Paisley handed each of the students a tablet notebook and instructed them to follow the onscreen directions to encrypt the device with their unique fingerprint identifier.

"Dr. Bourne and I'll have access to anything you put on this computer, but no one else will. There is messaging software built in, however, only from each of you to both of us. In other words, the platform won't allow you to interact with anyone else in or outside of this project. So, don't expect to receive calls or messages from your friends to meet for a pint at Dredges, or to strike up a virtual relationship with your peers." Mallory paused to sip her coffee; she could see the hand on the handle was trembling, perhaps from the caffeine but more likely it was because she was excited. Consciously trying to calm her nerves, she slowly set the cup down on the table, eager to finish without having skipped something important.

She turned back to resume the instructions. "You can upload, but will only be able to view notes. I'll tell you now; we can also see when your status is *active*. Every session will be timestamped, so just keep this in mind if you are offsite accessing the project folder, that is to say, if you leave without properly checking out, or hack into the network somehow. I strongly advise you *not* to forget the procedure. If we see that you have left with the device and or accessed the system, you can be assured of your prompt removal from the project."

"This is pretty serious."

"It is, Nigel," Paisley reinforced.

"Fifth and final point, more rules may apply later," Mallory said finally.

"Grey, I've assigned you to be Dr. Jacks's personal assistant, unless you have an objection?"

Grey McKnight shook his brown-haired, shaggy head. "I have not a one." His face remained expressionless while his gaze focused attentively on Dr. Jacks, although Dr. Bourne asked the question. Mallory bestowed a thin smile of acknowledgment. Grey situated himself further back into the folding chair, and hunched his broad shoulders forward, bowing his head. The chair squeaked under his giant frame.

"We'll expect you to keep India and Nigel informed of what she needs for them to be doing on any given day or to relay news that she may not have sent a team message about. She may also ask you to send messages on our behalf. Your device has been modified to allow you to send messages to them, but you will still not be able to receive India's and Nigel's replies."

"All right now … rather than me trying to explain what, exactly, all this is about let's take the rest of the conversation to the pit." Mallory said, masking her impatience with the blunt directive.

"I have just one question," India interjected. "For us three, this is our dissertation project. If we can't talk about it or even access the data outside of here how will we fulfil our school requirements?"

"My apologies, I should have clarified that point sooner. Dr. Jacks and I were counting on you three remaining so she made a quick call to notify the department of our temporary confidentiality requirements. We were offered the following solution. Rather than weekly status reports to your academic advisor and a final presentation, you will be able to publish a thesis upon completion of this excavation or when we make it public ourselves. As we have confirmation of your continued participation in this project, she can now call to confirm this arrangement."

"Although … we haven't told you anything yet, so you can still decide if you'd *rather* submit reports to your uni professor and make a presentation versus writing a thesis paper. In which case, you'd leave us to join another project that does not have the same restrictions." Mallory further clarified.

"Can we just submit reports to you and do a presentation at the end? I mean, *must* it be a thesis paper?" Nigel asked.

"To put it plainly, no," Mallory rejoined. Upon seeing

what she assumed was a quixotic expression on Nigel's face, she elaborated. "It cannot be a presentation and yes, it must be a thesis because I shan't take time away from *my* actual job to review your reports or play advisor. Please don't forget, I am not, nor is Dr. Bourne, affiliated with the university in any way. You can ask me all the questions you want; I may or may not answer them and that's where I draw the line in my responsibility to you as students. You will just have to think of yourselves as my employees. In return for employment, you are getting experience instead of a paycheque and while I can mentor, I cannot be your teacher. I am not qualified for that role.

"Also, Nigel, a presentation usually requires photography, CAD drawings of the dig site, and other technical specifications. These shan't be made available to you. First and foremost, this is a scientific project, not your personal soapbox for career advancement, although your work here can definitely help you in that direction. So again, knowing what you do, it is what it is, and a yay or nay will do."

From Mallory's forthright manner, which was typical, along with the extra measures, the doctors succeeded in piquing their team's curiosity. There was little doubt anyone would abandon the project now. "Yes," each of the three students replied.

"Good, now let's go, my minions," she said smiling widely.

Outside of the tent, the wind blustered past and whipped everyone's hair into a frenzy. The walk to the pit was silent; the only sound was that of five pairs of feet brushing over the lawn before they reached the grassless area. Mallory descended the ladder first, and then Paisley was followed by the others. "Nigel, remove the stakes from that side." Dr. Jacks pointed. Rolling it up, she calmly set the crumpled tarp inside the bucket.

"What the heck is that, a mastodon or something?" India asked upon its reveal while Mallory stomped on the covering with one quick thrust of her booted foot.

"It's bone, that's for sure," Nigel suggested.

Crouching on his haunches, Grey studied the exposed area. "It is a *human* bone, femur looks like."

"Bullocks," Nigel proclaimed.

"But not from any hominid species we've ever seen," Paisley volunteered. Ignoring Nigel, she cast a quick sidelong glance at her partner.

"This means, you may be right, Dr. Jacks. If we set aside the dimensions of this creature, since he or she was presumably placed within proximity, … henge *can be* burial sites. Was it sacrificed here? We have to wonder." Grey's eyes searched hers for confirmation. Instead of affirming immediately, she glanced at him questioningly.

"Seems impossible its human. It can't be. That bone is the size of my whole arm and as thick as my leg," India said.

"This is some kind of sham," Nigel interjected, having nothing more useful to offer.

Again, this time, Mallory seemed not to hear Nigel except at the very end. "You're right India; we can't tell for sure what it is until we uncover the entire specimen or more of it. But Grey is correct, as well. Right now, it appears to be human."

The four stood quietly studying and pondering the enormous bone. "All right, cover it up. Be gentle. Tomorrow, bright and early, together we'll continue working to expose this beast, and yes, Nigel, possibly a very creative dupe."

Half in Clay

†

MALLORY SENT INDIA and Nigel home for the day and Paisley left as well. Inside the admin tent, she rolled the portable radiator next to a chair and turned it on. "I won't keep you long," she said, dragging the chair closer and across from where Grey was already seated.

"I don't mind," he said, running his fingers through wavy brown hair. His eyes were wide and alert, but a shade darker and flatter than their normal multifaceted green.

She sat down and leaned forward, cocking her head to look directly into his eyes. "Grey, you're not staying after school because you did anything wrong."

"I know." He wiped a hand across his upper lip, seeming to conceal a grin.

"All right, so what made you think that the bone was human?" She leaned back into her seat and crossed her arms over her chest, folding one leg over the other, as well.

He clasped his hands in front of him, propping his elbows on his knees. "Maybe I didn't mention before that I have taken up a dual concentration: anthropology and palaeontology. It's in my school file, but I don't know if you have access to it."

"No, I didn't know and I don't have your file. I just call the school and they send me students who qualify, but I did ask for you this time."

"You did. Anyway, that piece seems human in its shape, especially. Every joint in animal bones is different since animals do not move like humans. Regardless of the creature, skeletal structure is not just a frame for the body; each bone is engineered for its use. Certain ones are thinner, more fragile, and less dense. Others are heftier to withstand pressure or weight. However, bones can also be the exact opposite of what you'd expect. A long thin one can be ten times as dense as a large porous one. Human bones are designed for human use and animal architecture is built specifically for them," he explained.

"And what differentiates our specimen from other primates then? Perhaps what we've uncovered is an ancestor of the great ape."

"Particularly, in this case, I know it's not a great ape specimen because not one of the other hominid species, past or present, naturally walked or *walks* upright. The bone in the pit is more bulbous at the top and bottom than that of an ape, its purpose to hinge securely in adjoining sockets at the correct angle. And still, the shaft has to be dense enough to be able to take the full weight of the body on it while distributing the pressure evenly. Otherwise, it would break."

"Good deductions, I guess we'll find out if you're right. Now, I'd also like to hear your thoughts on how stone circles were used."

"I think there is more to it, in general than it just having been a gathering place. We know ancient societies practiced some questionable pagan rituals, such as sacrifices of more than just your average fatted calf. We also know that throughout documented history, churches have been erected with graveyards. The logic being souls were forgiven of their sins, perhaps perceived as blessed when their bodily graves were placed in consecrated grounds. So, if we connect the two ideas it makes sense that the circles were holy places for the ancients—no different from the edifices we call churches even today."

Mallory was impressed. Keeping her face expressionless, she enquired further. "And for a student of paleoanthropology, how did you come to these conclusions?"

He brushed a hand through his hair again and looked nervously toward the tent entryway. They had never been alone together, but as far as Mallory knew, her company was not so intolerable that a person would wish to speedily escape it. "Grey?" Perhaps he had somewhere else to be. Hadn't he said, he didn't mind this impromptu meeting?

"Without sounding like a stalker, I know everything I can know about you. But it's only because I admire you and I agree with your hypotheses."

"You mean you've been following my work. That's great. I'm glad it inspires you," she encouraged gently. "You have the aptitude, but there's no need to feel uncomfortable with that just because right now the ideas are not your own. We all learn from our forebears and mentors. Just, for example, I wasn't the one to discover that henge were community centres. So, you might one day take a previously accepted concept and turn it on its head completely."

"Yes," he replied shortly.

She hesitated, waiting for him to expound. She had said to the others that she wasn't their teacher or advisor, but Grey was different. He was that once in a lifetime student with the mental capacity to astound and succeed if he opened his mind to the possibilities. She could sense the potential in him and wanted to help in the achievement of his goals, but he didn't seem to want her advice. Looking down at her wristwatch, she said, "All right then, have a good evening. Thanks for staying back and I'll see you tomorrow." She could not refrain from adding, "Among the safe company of others."

There was a flicker of a grin on his face. When they both came to a standing position at the same time, he quite suddenly stepped forward into narrow the gap between them, encircled her in his arms, bent down, and kissed her. She did not resist initially, instead, she let the instant heat penetrate her senses and skin. Finally, with a sliver of cognition, she pushed against his chest and he released her.

At a loss for words, she stared into his eyes. They were a still darker tint, but there was a glimmer in them now. His brows arched momentarily in question, provoking her to mirror the expression. She hadn't seen that coming, nor would she have imagined for a moment his aloof manner was for any reason other than it just being his way. *It was just a kiss*, she thought and worried. Regardless that Grey was not a teenager and she was *not* his teacher, she was still his boss, essentially.

"Just so you know, four years ago, I was an adjunct professor teaching Archaic Semiology at St. Ives College. That, as well, is probably in my student files."

"Seems it's me who didn't do the research."

Unconsciously she licked her lips.

"I've wanted to do that since the first day of the dig," he said softly, watching her.

"You've been planning to assault me for five weeks. Hmm, that's *not* normal ... just so you know—in case you regularly, professionally *admire* others. Yes, definitely crosses the invisible stalking line."

"Let's be honest, from your reaction I don't really think you thought I was assaulting you. And I didn't mean this project; the last excavation, two years ago ... when we first met."

Again, she was stunned. For as long as she could remember, Mallory was rather clueless about men; she knew this was a character flaw. Every romantic relationship thus far had been a casualty of her obliviousness and she tended not to think about it until it smacked her in the face. For example, a few weeks ago, she hadn't thought that that interlude with Keaton, when she was sixteen, still meant something—to either of them. Then offhandedly, Paisley said her brother had been in love with Mallory since she was fourteen years old. Now, Grey revealed that for two years he'd wanted to kiss her.

She stepped closer. "Just the once?"

John Doe

✝

THEY WERE IRRITATING; asking questions every few minutes, making annoying noises in between, getting up to stretch, or taking impromptu breaks for small talk. The specimen needed to be uncovered, but she would have to reassign these two to another pit. Possibly she would also need to request more helpers from the university to pick up the slack after Ambrose and Cara's departure. Mallory was not looking forward to preparing the newbies.

India inhaled audibly and then tittered at something Nigel said. "Dr. Jacks, is—?"

"Both of you just shut up," Grey muttered brusquely.

"Whoa, mate, we disturbing you?" He too, let out a mild snort, afterward brushing the underside of his nose with the back of his hand. The gesture resulted in a dirty streak slashed across his upper lip.

"Surprise surprise, another question. Now try and *observe* my answer," he said pointedly, glaring at Nigel. After an electric silence, Grey looked down and resumed his work.

"Dr. Jacks said we could ask questions and India is just trying to understand. Pardon us," Nigel sneered. "But I think we'll just let the *real boss* tell us what to do."

Mallory first cast Grey a cursory glance and noticed from his profile, his jaw was twitching. When she looked at India, the young woman was staring adoringly at her knight in dull armor. "Nigel, you have a moustache," India whispered, smiled crookedly, and sneezed.

The student scrubbed his nose and laughed. "India, you don't have to keep your voice down. You won't wake John Gigantopithecus Doe." She rolled her eyes and bobbed her head toward Grey, to which Nigel just grunted.

Mallory was still bent over her work but Nigel's attitude needed responding to; she resumed her scraping and said over the faint scratching sound, "Apart from your not so subtle bad work manners, you're both irritating me with whatever that sniffling noise is. If either or both of you has caught a cold, take it home. We'll be seeing you again in a couple of days." She looked up and grimaced at Nigel when he punctuated her comments with another sneeze. "Otherwise, I thought I made myself clear: I'm not a textbook and this is not a casual study session we've organised for your benefit. I think it best if, after today, you moved onto quadrant six."

"I'll stay right here if it's all the same …"

"Nigel, it's really more about what *I* would rather you be doing. So, you can pick up where Cara left off and chitchat there if you want, or spray the area with spit and snort to your heart's content. And maybe ask each other questions and try to conclude your own answers. However, since I'm looking for productivity here, I have half a mind to assign you to separate pits."

India had the decency to look embarrassed. Nigel's expression appeared more petulant and Grey's teeth were still clenched behind his lips.

The *boss's* two cents were obviously not penetrating the overall attitude of the group, especially Nigel's. Mallory tried another way. "Look, I think we all know this henge is special. No other excavation *ever* has revealed what we've found here. Let that sink in because I have a feeling there are unique artefacts to be found near the other stones as well. Apparently, you *think* I'm your primary school teacher. That's fine, for just long enough for you to hear this: you all have to alter your mindset, work together, or you'll be sent to the corner. Are we all finally on the same page?"

"Yes, and I'd like to continue working where I left off the day before yesterday if that's all right, number seven. Maybe I'll find something myself … that'll be exciting."

"Good idea, India. Now clean up that orbital socket and make some headway on the mandibular joint." The student made a twittering sound, like a small bird and bent over her task.

Mallory wondered about India and how she came to be drawn to Nigel. Before today, India frequently reminded Mallory of her mother. The small framed young woman with straight black hair pulled back in a ponytail, tanned skin, and a button nose was usually professional, serious but with a dry humor, and not so prone to giggles and speaking with her eyes. However, Anjali Nischal, as Mallory's mother was named before she married, might have been just as cutesy when she was in her twenties and being courted by Mallory Jacks, senior. Nevertheless, there was also something about India's mannerisms that brought Mrs. Jacks to mind; like the way she wore her watch face on her inner wrist and when she flipped her hand to look at the time, her thumb and index finger folded delicately toward one another.

Nigel, on the other hand, bore no fond personality or physical resemblance to Mr. Jacks. Granted, the validity of this comparison in the first place—solely based on India's minor similarities with Mallory's mother—was questionable. Regardless, instead of being magnetic and clever as Mallory's father had been, Nigel did not have exactly an aggressive demeanor, but rather a troublesome nature. His appearance comparatively was much more disheveled as well. He was wiry thin but wore slouchy clothing, which allowed him to comfortably slump further. His long face with its ordinary features tended to transform unattractively with various cynical or negative expressions, even when his comments were seemingly banal.

If Mallory could have exchanged any of her helpers, despite Ambrose's lack of real interest, she would have opted for him over Nigel. Ambrose, at least, focused on his tasks when doing them, never pretended at being something he wasn't—an established know-it-all, merely in school to claim the credentials rightfully owed him, that is—and he refrained from challenging his peers, who were students too. Ironically, Ambrose required less of her attention than some of the other graduate students she'd managed, of course, present company included.

"Confirming, John here is a Gigantopithecus. Right?"

"Nigel, seriously, I want you to go home every evening and write down a list of questions you have—"

"Great, works for me," he interrupted.

Mallory continued, "Then spend an hour or so searching for answers online. If you don't find what you're looking for I'll answer them. But, I'll want a list of resource links or a bibliography of the print materials where you've looked. And as I said, going forward you'll definitely be working in pit six." She realized these instructions meant more work for her—in checking those resources—but she had no intention of actually expending that effort and knew Nigel didn't either.

He sneezed internally, making a gross phlegmatic sound. "I think I need tomorrow off." Quietly he stood up, depositing his brush and pickax into a bucket. Then he came back to lean down and whisper something in India's ear. Next, hovering over his work-study sponsor until she cranked her head to look up, he said, "Come to think of it, I don't feel wonderful right now. I'm going home."

"Dr. Jacks, I don't feel well either. I think we've both caught something like you said," India said weakly.

"Fine, but leave your tablets with Dr. Bourne. Get well soon. I need you."

Nigel had begun to walk away after Mallory's "Fine." India nodded and apologized for getting sick before following her boyfriend.

Grey shook his head. "Ah, the comforting sound of silence. I hate to say this but I think you'll need a new strategy. I heard Nigel complaining yesterday that he doesn't want to do a thesis paper and he was going to try to get you to change your mind. He showed up today with a high-res camera."

"Well, damn! But he hasn't had the opportunity to snap any shots today. I'm sure he meant to talk to me first."

"I went into his bag and delivered the camera to Dr. Bourne. … Let's just say it was a precautionary measure."

"Good thinking. Sneaky bugger. I'm going to run over there right now and make sure they turned in their tablets and if they didn't then I'll have Paiz, Dr. Bourne, wipe the devices. Might be a while, I have to call for more recruits too. Was planning to do that anyway and this time, I'll have the new students work on the stones. The fewer who know about this guy the better." She stood and dusted off her pants. "Think of a name for him, why don't you?"

"The cut of his jaw, he looks like an Adam to me," he said, grimacing and tilting his head sideways to peer into the cavernous giant's eyes. "But then the original Adam was only, oh, a diminutive bloke of about four metres half, according to someone, I forget, or maybe he was twenty-seven metres tall—sixty cubits as suggested in the Quran. Maybe we should call him Goliath and stay on the safe side of inaccuracy. Since Adam was a more popular figure, I doubt whether the sources of those estimations would quibble over a couple dozen metre discrepancy."

"Goliath. Sounds about right," Mallory said, pleased with Grey's cursory assessment of the subject's height at being a minimum of fifteen feet. "Gah-li," she said flatly, pulling back to the root of her American accent. "It's an expression of awe in the US. Golly is fitting; don't you think?"

Earth Quaking

†

IT WAS PAST mid-afternoon of the third day after finding the femur bone. They had picked and brushed away enough debris to completely reveal the surface portion of the head and one leg. However, the need to progress was overwhelming the thrill of discovery. The astounding humanesque figure was seventeen feet five inches in length, measuring from the heel of his foot to the crown of his head. Golly's breadth could not yet be determined. His shoulders and torso were slightly angled and still both entirely embedded in the compact earth.

At roughly five meters or seventeen feet from ground level, the stone loomed in the center of the pit in a crusty, mud-covered mass. Mallory tasked Grey with removing the dirt from the surface of the henge stone while she continued to uncover Golly's remains. It would have been easier to wash the stone, but drenching the ground of the pit, along with it the skeleton, was not an option.

Overhead the scaffold rattled and a bucket fell and bounced away. Instinctively, she pulled herself away from the skeleton, gripped the tool in her hand, and scanned the pit. The earth remained steady; it was not a tremor. Whipping her head, she squinted up at Grey. "Careful!"

The small of his back was braced against the railing behind

him, and yet, he teetered backward slightly over the same metal pipe. With his arms splayed to either side, he stood there absolutely still, clasping the bar of the parapet. She could see the stark white tension in the knuckles of his fingers as well as the taut muscles along his arms.

"What happened? You all right?" She asked calmly, shielding her eyes from the sun. "You caused a minor quake."

"I— I'm … yuh— you might want to come up here."

Scaling the side, she hoisted herself onto the six-foot high platform, stood next to him, and perused the stone surface. Less than two feet above where he was standing, on the left most of the stone face, was a deep engraving: a perfect cutout of a man. The figure was furthermore surrounded by wings that were more so burnished onto the stone than carved. She walked past Grey to take a closer look. Approximately ten inches tall, the figure itself looked machine crafted—the outer edge was precise, the depth was uniform throughout except for at the center of its chest, and the shape's dimensions seemed to be proportionate to a modern human's. Amidst its torso area, was another symbol in relief: an eye. To complete the picture, the entire figure hovered over a nondescript elliptical shape.

Mallory put a hand to her chest, to calm her thumping heart as she turned to glance up at Grey. He was still leaning backward, although his elbows now rested against the railing. He looked shocked certainly but almost frightened as well.

"A common motif," he muttered; his complexion pale. He pressed his lips together after these few words but his eyes glowed unnaturally as though electrified. "The eye … used by many cultures and faiths to depict a wide variety of ideas outside of the realms of realistic sight … the Omnipotent and Omnipresent, lunar or solar direction, self-spirituality, and even prophetic vision, for example," he expounded cautiously.

"What about that scares you? You practically threw yourself off the platform and you're not exactly recovered, are you?"

It was his turn to stare at her. Tentatively he released his grip on the rail and embraced her instead, almost as though jumping off a narrow ledge into her arms. "I'm afraid … I'm too afraid to tell you that at the moment," he said, resting his chin on the top of her head. "But for some reason, you make me feel a whole lot safer."

"Work getting done down there or are you just taking a break?"

Pulling away, Mallory glanced up toward the voice and said, "Pa—, Grey's made a new discovery. I'm— we're coming out; we need to talk."

"Should I wait here for you?" Paisley asked.

"No … need a few minutes."

"All right, you know where I shall be," she said, walking back presumably toward the artifacts tent. Although all discussions we held in the administrative tent, Dr. Bourne's daily work was done in the other structure.

"Grey, it's shocking but it's also all right. Get a hold of yourself," Mallory said smiling.

"Mm, yes, shocking."

She rose on her tiptoes and traced the outline of the figure with her finger. Grey stood watching her curiously, as though she were attempting some feat of bravery. "Get my camera …

in my bag." While the student descended the parapet, she extracted the broad bristle brush from her back pocket and leaned toward the stone, propping herself against it with the fingertips of her left hand. Even though she had learned professional patience over the years, in the irresistible hope of catching a glimpse of more symbols beneath the surface crust of dirt, she wafted the area above the carving as far as she could reach with the brush. Of course, the effort was fruitless; the layer of dried mud was too thick.

When Grey returned, she captured a few awkwardly angled pictures herself before he took the camera from her hands and snapped a couple more. Together, they rapidly toggled the snapshots through the digital display. The images would suffice to show Paisley, but better ones would need to be captured later when the scaffold was raised further and the tripod could be setup.

They climbed down the parapet, crossed the pit, and up the ladder to ground level. Beside her, relative to modern human terms, Grey's enormous frame stalked toward the collections tent unspeaking; neither did she say anything. However, it was likely they were thinking about the same thing—the find was intriguing after all. Mallory was also preoccupied with the logistics of the project going forward, but in the back of her mind, she wondered why Grey reacted the way he did.

Everything about this case was big. The colossal stones, the skeletal remains of a giant, even every piece of news, from the day the one stone was found to now, was tremendous in terms of its impact on the field of anthropology.

Twenty or so feet from the doorway, Grey halted but Mallory kept walking. He reached out, grabbing her arm. Tenuously he questioned, "Would you go out with me, despite our student-teacher relationship? Say, this evening we could go have a drink and maybe dinner somewhere quiet?"

"What do you mean ... romantic-like?"

"You can't have forgotten. We kissed. So yes, that's what I'm implying."

"Grey," she intoned hesitantly. "I'm no good on that front."

"What front would that be? Relationships with students, relationships in general, drinking in intimate settings, or drinking in general? I presume you eat and sometimes around other people." He wasn't smiling, but she could hear the teasing humor in his voice.

"This might come as a bit of a shock, but all of the above. Although, I meant more that a woman is often blamed for walking into something aware, but still with some crazy notion that she can change a man to suit her idea of what would make that relationship perfect. I, on the other hand, have a tendency toward inspiring the reverse effect. Frankly, you'd have to either be satisfied with a casual thing or accept that, eventually, you'll be disappointed. Not disappointed in *that* way—" she corrected, blushing a tinge. What a fool thing to say, she thought. She ducked her head in embarrassment and blurted, "*We* won't go anywhere ... if you're hoping for an actual long-term situation."

"Hm." Lowering his gaze, he pawed the ground with his foot. "If I saw your name and number on a lavatory wall, 'Call for a good time,' then you'd oblige for the short term, but asking you out to dinner I run the risk of being shunned if our whatever relationship is prolonged?" He looked up, his stare colliding with hers.

She peered at him through narrowed eyes. "You overstep. That's not what I meant and you know it. I can't give you a better warning than the one I already have."

"I was nervous to ask and no wonder. As it's turned out, this has been the most complex initial date proposal in the history of my first date proposals. So now that I have been duly forewarned and am willing to take the risk, is it finally a date? Oh, and rest easy, I can't imagine there's anything about you that I would think needs changing *for me*. I like you exactly as you are."

His softened facial expression and the admission that went along with it was entirely too forthright and made her feel minutely uncomfortable. He didn't seem cognizant of the warning, although he'd acknowledged it. "If you can remember our working partnership comes first, then fine," she remarked. Life would take its natural course and he would learn or maybe, she was just taking his simple question too seriously. "And while I don't really think of you as a student now, you're still my lackey." She smirked. "I expect your diligence in that regard not to change."

"Fine," he said, now grinning. "During work hours, I'll make sure your coffee is perfect, one sugar and one creamer, and never just lukewarm. For *non*-working times, I'll think of some other way to serve—sometime after our first date, of course."

Nodding prematurely, notwithstanding her usual lack of comprehension when it came to innuendo, she blushed again.

Well, Golly

†

BRUPTLY GLANCING AT her watch, Mallory rushed forward into the tent. "India! But, ehm, you're still sick." She covered her nose and mouth with her hands. "I hate colds, go home this minute, you're contagious."

"I'm not, Dr. Jacks." The student smiled and gestured a downward hand wave, signaling Mallory could uncover her face. "Turned out to be an allergic reaction to Nigel's cologne, that he was allergic to as well, but didn't know it until I came along and started sneezing during, um … exertion."

"But he's not here and your nose is still very red."

"That's because of him too, but the imbecile part. I won't go into all of that; it wouldn't be very professional of me. Anyway, I'd like to resume work. Please, can I come back? I'm committed, I promise. I don't know why I let him influence me, must be getting desperate in my old age." She laughed a pleasant tinkling kind of laugh. "He won't be coming back and I won't have anything more to do with him."

"We had a feeling … and of course, you can pickax where you left off." Mallory couldn't help herself when it came to her one-way game of puns with India. The student's lips puckered with mirth. "I'm glad we didn't lose you. We wiped your tablet, however."

"Dr. Jacks, Nigel told some people you uncovered a prehistoric ape."

"Yes, Keaton called," Paisley announced. She tapped the touchscreen of her laptop and navigated to the project folders on the network, scooting a device meant for India closer. The screen of the smaller device blinked, the LEMM logo appeared, and a progress bar indicating that data was being uploaded began to move.

India pressed her thumb on the screen. "He had the chance to voice it, I know, but he was pretty miffed about having to change his program requirements for this project … thought it was unfair that you changed the rules after the fact," she continued. "I told him he was being arrogant. As you said, our work study is not a priority on the scale of things and you'd actually accommodated us more than expected by clearing the thesis option with our college."

"Thanks, India. That's what I was coming to tell you, Dr. Jacks. Nevertheless, nothing to worry about, at this point." Once the device was restored and connected, Paisley swiped sideways to the next interface and entered preliminary credentials: the project name, today's date, user name, and a four-digit identifier. Then swiping again, she nudged the computer toward the student for her fingerprint to be entered in the blank box. Within a couple of seconds, "Successful Entry" appeared on India's device to confirm the completion of the setup process.

"Right, because did Nigel have proof to back his claim? I don't think so. Makes no difference to me, we gave him the opportunity to back out, and I can assure you he'll be even more upset when he gets the wind of what's been sacrificed in exchange. Let's just move on. I was thinking on my way over here that everything about this case is big." Mallory toggled the camera menu to the display the thumbnails and navigated to the latest pictures taken, passing the camera to Paisley.

"It's about four metres from the ground on the left edge of the West face of the stone. Dr. Bourne, I think we need to call in the reserves, so to speak. We have barely grazed the surface of the other twelve henge stones. I doubt whether we've just gotten lucky finding all this in the first pit we started on. The fact is, we four know this is a breakthrough discovery … now that we've uncovered Golly, I'm also wondering whether it need be a secret any longer and we shouldn't get other teams in here. What do you think? The majority of student recruits are not dependable." Holding the camera close to her face, she studied the clearest image of the etching. "At this rate, we'll never get to analysis. One good thing is we don't have to send this out, Grey is a bona fide semiologist."

"That's great news; I'm all the more thankful to have you on our team, Grey," Paisley said appreciatively.

"Really—you can translate hieroglyphics?" India asked awe-fully.

"Egyptian symbolism is not my area of expertise; I can only decipher meaning somewhat. I'm rather more of a generalist," he explained.

"Could you say offhand what cultural influences are at play in this depiction? I don't think I've ever seen this sort of iconography in relation to the Celtic pagans," Mallory asked him.

He hesitated, nervously running his fingers through his hair as she had seen him do before. "I mentioned the eye motif is common. It is thought to have originated in early Egyptian civilizations and is used even today on currency from the United States, for example. The figure and wings could be connected with Celtic beliefs, fairies, pixies, and the like. The Welsh dragon folklore might have something to do with it as well, the human in the foreground signifying the tamer of such a beast. I'd have to look into it much further, that's just my cursory assessment. We'd have to determine first the age of the circle and then try and pinpoint the community that constructed it, in order to get a better handle."

"Ah yes, first things ..." Paisley acknowledged. "Aly, Dr. Jacks, as to that, I agree we need hands, but if we make this announcement to the professional community, the site will be overrun with gapers as well as those who want a piece of anthropological history making. I foresee us having even a tougher time with who to allow and who to turn away—never mind that I haven't budgeted for security.

"You three concentrate on pit one and I'll confer with the LEMM board and try to find a solution. I haven't yet told them what we've found. Instead, I've perpetuated the belief it's just an ordinary excavation and will continue to do that while posing the question of how to get help since the project is so large. I'll let you know what we come up with."

"If I may interject a thought here as well?"

"Certainly, Grey," said Paisley, twirling a pencil between her fingers thoughtfully.

"If you know of a colleague who might be able to organise just the dig resources—"

"Yes, but the dilemma would be the same. Hordes of uninvited acclaim seekers will show up," Paisley interrupted.

"One person who you trust," when Mallory opened her mouth to speak, he raised his voice slightly, "*who* knows how to guide a team *just so far*. Then we can get the bulk of the useless materials hauled out without anyone else, except your confidant, having to know anything more than what you tell him or her. The overburden is done with, but from pit one we know there isn't anything really until four metres below that. The earth could be run through a sifter just to make sure before it's hauled away. As for the remaining surface, an experienced person—with your added guidance, of course—would know when to tell the diggers to stop. Given that all trash is valuable, you'd just have to be all right with possibly missing the odd throwaway, likely a modern age doing anyway, I would think."

"You mean with a crew we could tackle all the pits at once, a linear stage strategy. Dr. Bourne, that could work," Dr. Jacks said hopefully.

"It could, yes." Paisley took a moment long to consider Grey's suggestion. "So, someone I trust implicitly and who would get a charge out of just such a case, maybe even if the only information he is given is anticipatory … The bizarre part is none of us have any theories on what Golly is … which could work for us. I wouldn't have to lie, or conceal much, as it turns out. Thank you, Grey. I didn't think of it that way. I just happen to know this person you described. However, for now, the most important thing, or things rather, are what you've found already and making progress."

"Sorry to interrupt, but Golly?" India questioned.

"Goliath, we've named him," Grey supplied. "Golly is a shortened name for the very tall man." He frowned in consternation as if realizing the connection for the first time even though Mallory had mentioned it before. "I once met an American and she exclaimed the same to me, 'Well, golly, you're a tall man.' "

"And that's another thing, we don't even know definitively if *it* is a *he*. What we do know is Neolithic constructions above ground were not uncommon, but the strata in which we found Golly places him square in the prehistoric period, at the very least," Mallory stated.

"That can't be right," India pronounced.

"Indeed, there is something wrong with the picture. I mean something else, apart from the fact that we've found a giant. Regardless, 6000BCE collectively would be my guess, which would also make Gwellen's henge the oldest uncovered to date. See what I mean? Everything about this project will have a colossal impact."

Everything's a Sell

†

MALLORY WENT HOME to shower, change clothes, brush her hair, and put on glossy lip-salve. That was as far as her 'date' preparations usually went. As an added measure, she swiped a few strokes of a mascara wand across her eyelashes.

Handsome as Grey was, she was all too aware, he was also a graduate student. Yet, there was a magnetic quality about him she had not experienced before with other men. Even with the ease in the friendship between herself and Keaton, there existed an invisible cord holding her back from making more of the relationship than it was. Although she hadn't analyzed the bond, any attraction she felt now was perhaps subconsciously restrained because he was Paisley's brother.

She recollected how she had readily thought of Grey when the Gwellen project was in its infant stages. The image of 'Grey McKnight' underlined numerous times on a page of her notebook was ingrained in her mind. *Strange*, she thought, how she had asked the anthropology department at the university for him, specifically. Still remembering his full name after two years was telling; she generally wasn't very good with names.

Her parents died shortly after that project. She recalled that as well. The day had been like any other, except that it was Thursday—family dinner night. She would arrive at her parents' house—her current residence and home now—directly after work and help her mother make dinner. She would tell them a new little something about work, relay stories, and her parents would do the same. Mallory Senior would joke at his daughter's expense and Anjali would defend her by teasing her husband in return. That dinner was missed; the last time she'd seen them alive was the Thursday before. She thought back to the occasion with a tiny smile plastered on her face.

Although they rarely inquired, her father had asked her outright if she had an "official" boyfriend. Her mother said before Mallory could reply, "What your father is saying, somewhat sideways, is we hope you have a *new* one because James is un-British. What sort of man asks for a coffee with a handsome dollop of Amaretto—'if we have it'—when only offered tea? Premium Darjeeling, no less."

Blinking back the sharp sting of sudden tears, she resumed her ministrations, picking off tiny clumps of mascara from her lashes. She didn't want to look as though a spindly-legged spider sat atop her eyelids, which of course is not at all how the softly accentuated eyes appeared in the mirror. However, not wearing any cosmetics at all usually, oddly made her more self-conscious of her appearance, as though she was shouting, "Hey, look at me. I made myself pretty for you."

Just after seven o'clock in the evening, she arrived at Mantra, a much-loved neighborhood Indian restaurant, another reminder of her beautiful mother. Regardless of its popularity, the small family-run establishment inspired a refined crowd of diners. The soft twangs of sitar music, which emanated from invisible surround-sound speakers, filling the space; the torchiere lighting and candles that muted the vibrantly colored decor; and the sweet smell of jasmine plants intermingling with distinctly Indian cooking spices, all imposed an intimate, even sensual ambiance.

Rounding the hallway toward the hostess's desk, Mallory identified her would-be companion, pointing at him when asked if she had a reservation. With his long legs stretched out beside a round corner table constructed of some rattan-type weave, he sat in a matching woven chair. She didn't hear what the familiar hostess said, but when the young woman gestured toward the table, as though to show her the way, Mallory smiled cursorily. "Promise I won't get lost, Rupa," she commented and proceeded to walk past her. When she approached, Grey stood; towering over her—making her feel suddenly even smaller than her already petite self. A tiny electric jolt squeezed her heart when he smiled. Involuntarily, her brow furrowed and his smile disappeared only to return when she forcibly un-creased her forehead.

For the first twenty minutes of their date, they talked about work since she was an awkward conversationalist when it came to more trivial topics. Primarily, this was because she didn't often participate in other, what would be deemed 'normal,' social activities. For one, she didn't feel the need to be entertained and second, nor would she socialize for the sake of it. This childhood development had permeated into every aspect of her adult life. It wasn't for any bitterness she carried; she just abhorred being pandered too and that was what she classified most entertainment as. Even in private, Mallory rarely watched television—with it being her philosophy to avoid commercials if possible. Whenever she turned on her TV nowadays, there just happened to be an advertisement playing on every channel as she flipped through. She'd have to sit through the commercial just to see if the actual show was something she wanted to watch. The cable guide told her the title and so once or twice, she waited through the sales pitch. A few minutes later into the show, another advert would interrupt and here was where she lost patience for the next few weeks. As she flicked off the tube, she invariably thought: Oh, did you really want chips with your malt vinegar?

She and Keaton had had several discussions about the commercialism of news, too. Having also long believed that most media was more biased than it claimed to be, from these conversations with him, she learned she wasn't alone in this perspective. In fact, it was this discovery of the nature of journalism that had stymied his ambitions of youth. He had once wanted a national and even global stomping ground, perhaps even the acclaim to go with it. Instead, both she and Keaton practiced selective awareness. However, it was unfortunate that even the driest of informative programs contained a smattering of advertisements nowadays; but after Paisley explained that advertising *was* funding even for news venues, Mallory deemed a few adverts were excusable. Still, she noted the tolerable, ten-second "notes from our sponsor" were now just teasers; once engrossed in the program the ads ran much longer.

Spiritual Matters

LL WELL AND good if we can wrap our heads around it," she said trying to sound casual. She looked around to make sure their conversation wasn't being overheard. "But there were no five-metre tall hominids in the Mesolithic period. If giant men ever existed, it would have been during the prehistoric age when everything was bigger … cockroaches the size of armadillos and giant men hunting dinosaurs for their supper." Even as she spoke, she assessed Grey. Albeit physically different, subconsciously she compared him to Keaton. What were Grey's philosophies and did he share her peculiarities?—she wondered.

"Or … if you consider the bible as a history book," Grey said cryptically, leaning forward, and folding his hands over one another. "But before we further submerge ourselves in the abyss of all that, I'd like to learn about you what I *haven't* gathered from your CV or bits-n-bobs from here and there."

She chewed the bottom of her lip, considering how one went about describing herself on a personal level.

"Are you a private person?"

Observing the placid expression on his face and the stillness of his body language, she tried to mirror his manner and give a thoughtful but calm answer to his question. "I suppose I am, but not because I particularly go out of my way to hide, rather, I am just not very public. Most of the time, I see socialising as something requiring effort and with little purpose. If it means schmoozing, apart from the company of a few people, arrogant as it sounds, I prefer my own. And it might be macabre to say, but in many ways, I'm much like a found object in my work; a fossil that has a story and holds value to someone, but isn't noticed until it's uncovered."

"A priceless gemstone."

"Grey …" His name lingered as she glared at him, instead seeing in her mind's eye, a hook dangling before her. Suspiciously, she wondered what more he was *trying* to lure her toward; they were already on a date. She was not immune to flirtations and his advances, in particular, were welcome, although she didn't know why. However, she might have to warn him again that perhaps his tactics were a touch over the top. "I'd like to hear the pickup lines you use on women who do not liken themselves to artefacts. I would think the 'diamond in the rough' approach would come off as insulting to most." She batted her eyelashes.

Acknowledging the jibe with only a grin he continued. "Were you closer to your mother or father?"

"That's a tough question. And not because by answering I would feel I was betraying one by choosing the other. A brief answer would just be a fragment of the truth. Offhand, I would say, I was closer to my father. Now don't ask me which one of them I miss more or who I would have thrown a life preserver to had I been given the chance of saving only one of them from a drowning Titanic." Her chest felt tight. Every time she spoke of them, it was hard to contain the flood of emotion she felt.

She didn't really have anyone with whom she voiced her grief (or joyful memories). Paisley would listen and be sympathetic but she never asked and Mallory needed the prompting. Her parents, their life and their death, were topics she could not boldly request they discuss. She understood why Paisley didn't bring it up; her friend knew that while remembering was good, the reminders were also painful. The one absolute Mallory knew about her best friend was that she was incapable of causing, let alone abetting pain. It would hurt Paisley to do so.

He nodded, tilting his head. "Which of them are you more like?" he asked softly, watching the server place the dishes they'd ordered on the table between them on a Lazy Susan, arranging the petal shaped stainless steel saucers in the pattern of a flower. After the waiter left, Grey took a long draft from an emblematized Kingfisher beer glass and then reached over the table for Mallory's plate.

"Does this question answer session only move in one direction—you question; I answer? Tamarind or cilantro chutney or the mango pickle? Ehm, that doesn't count as an interview question."

"For now, yes, and all three, thanks." He reached over and took the proffered condiment caddy. "My story shan't make sense in parts, or you'd have to be psychic to catch on to the meaningful parts." Expertly, with two fingers and the thumb of his right hand he tore off a piece of the warm nan. "Are you more like your mother or father?"

"I am more like my father, that's probably why I loved my mother just the same, in truth, if not a little more. My father was my friend and my mother ... I admired. From both I've inherited so much besides what someone might think are my ordinary physical features and my paltry worldly possessions." This second question, while still difficult was easier for the simple reason of it being a sort of relief.

"Beauty is in the eye of the beholder, as whoever once said, and I behold that you are anything but ordinary," he said solemnly.

"Regardless of my comment … my appearance is apart from the point I was trying to make. I was only illustrating that inheritance goes much deeper than what the eye can see. I agree it's really about perception, but that comes after the fact. At first glance, everyone is either special or ordinary, as judged in a naturally human way by someone else. The difference is because I really knew them I considered them both beautiful in their way. They've bestowed some of that to me and I am grateful." Her eyes watered slightly in fond remembrance and she sniffled. The spices in the chicken tikka masala and palak paneer were doing a fine job of clearing her sinuses as well and she was thankful for the convenience.

"Is that science or do you attribute those gifts to something else?" he posed next.

"Both, nature and nurture. As far as I've heard there isn't conclusive evidence that genetic inheritance influences personality, but then not even the most reputable scientist could convince me that the sense of humor my dad and me shared, for example, wasn't biologically linked somehow. Yet, I'm one-hundred percent certain that there's no *love* gene." She smiled to herself and looked up to find him watching her intently. She was having a nice time, she realized. Surprisingly, it hadn't taken much effort at all to get over the impersonal nature of their usual teacher/student relationship. This conversation was very personal and yet intriguing, albeit still more one-sided than she would have preferred. Grey was easy to talk to, and the fact that she found herself readily elaborating with her answers made her feel more at ease than did his compliments.

By now the last of the entrees were devoured. Sensing the sweat on her upper lip, she dabbed around her mouth with a napkin. "Medium plus" translated over differently this time; maybe the chefs had made the dishes even spicier than she usually liked. Although a sweet dessert of gulab jamun would calm the palate, she couldn't fathom eating another bite. She reclined back in her seat against the embroidered, silk sari pillow and nursed a glass of refreshing water.

"Since we've moved on to the subject of science and the unseen, do you think that science can include creationism? Is it inherent for an anthropologist to be an evolutionist, or plainly, does the philosophy of religion enter *your* interpretation of science?"

Nothing was as satisfying as guzzling cold water after a spicy meal, but that inevitably led to an uncomfortable bloated feeling within seconds. Sipping the water slowly, as her mother had taught her, she peered over the rim of the glass at her composed companion before answering. "I think of genetics as a science in the here and now, in other words, just one of the many studies that mankind conducts ... of processes already in existence." She paused and shifted in her seat. Grey was a student of anthropology and he would probably find out himself that religion and this science were incongruous topics, at least when it came to the individual. It was all right to study the religious practices and beliefs of old, but beyond that, actual faith-based philosophy had no place with credible scientific analysis, especially amongst a person's career goals in this field. Unless you were an ecclesiastic, it was better to keep your beliefs and opinions separate and to yourself if you hoped to be taken seriously.

"I know why you hesitate but we're just talking. Please, go on."

Trying to fathom his reasoning for this line of questioning, she looked piercingly into his eyes for a moment. Seeing nothing untoward in his gaze back, she answered. "Well, science, to me, *is* creationism; since we do not create anything simply by studying it, rather the reverse, it exists and then we investigate how it came to be. In my metaphysical heart, I know all sciences—including genetics and anthropology—to have a long history of inheritance that was passed down to us from somewhere. We just don't know where yet.

"I find it hard to believe that *lifeless* particles mish-mashed together could miraculously form intelligent, complex, emotional *living* things, regardless of how much time evolution has had to do that. And then that's contradictory as well—to juxtapose miracles with science." She stared blankly at her date in wonderment of her own thoughts on the matter and then suddenly chuckled. "Have you ever seen one of those time-lapse videos of what an infant would look like in various stages of growth as it ages?"

"Mm-hm," he hummed, enraptured, but he did not smile

back.

"How come no brilliant scientist has been able to show the progression from atomic particles to a human being? Then, how did the primordial soup come to have a brain, and one that no less told it to laugh or cry based on very individualised stimuli? And while it may be common for anthropologists to ascribe to the theory of evolution, in my mind there is a difference between what one *learns* and then thinks, and what one *knows* by way of belief and then thinks. I don't profess to know everything, even about my area of expertise, but I know that no missing links have been found between the ape and a human. You would think we would have found one mid-evolutionary example of a part monkey part human. And now I'm certain, for we've found a giant before we've found even that."

The look on Grey's face was indescribable; there was no obvious sign of pleasure or displeasure at Mallory's lengthy reply, however, he must have been appeased for his green eyes seemed to progressively brighten and sparkle.

"And now let me ask you one last profound question: do you follow the dove or the raven? A strange one, to be sure, but we might as well get to the crux of the thing. There existed giants before the deluge and also after."

As the waiter cleared the table, delivered the check and Grey paid it, Mallory eyed him quixotically and reviewed, for a minute, the previous conversation. His beginning and last comments had come full circle and it had not escaped her notice that Grey had made sectarian references even before. She hoped for his sake that his interest was just trifling notions.

Dismissing the over analysis, she laughed again. "Grey, were you attempting to tell me through your line of questioning that you are a theologian as well as being a semiologist and a student of paleoanthropology?"

"You could say that, except I would make a minor correction. I've already said, possibly to the disappointment of some, as a semiologist, I'm a generalist." Bringing an index finger to his lips, thoughtfully he added, "For that matter, although a student of anthropology and paleontology, I'm not a trained theologian either—an apprentice of a lot and master of nothing."

"We're all the same, each of us knowing bits-n-bobs of this and that with very few pieces fitting together perfectly. Thanks for dinner, although making it wasn't your doing … for footing the tab, anyway, and I've appreciated the conversation." She leaned over and placed her hand over his—briefly caressing the top with her thumb before pulling away. "Another although though, I don't think I've learned much about *you*, except maybe that you're philosophical as well as being a good listener. I don't suppose you study reverse psychology as well. Because I am intrigued and hope we can do this again at some time, except with me being the one doing the interrogation." Rising precipitously from her seat, she rounded the chair and pushed it toward the table, suddenly mesmerized by a mysterious electric field enveloping them, casting the seated diners into a distant realm.

Grey stood as well and grasped her hand, swiftly entangling his fingers with hers. "You weren't going to leave me wondering about my last question, were you?"

Turning to face him, she cranked her head upward, looking into his eyes as she answered, "Dove or raven? A biblical reference, I assume and of which's meaning I am not certain that I can attest to with confidence." Of a mind, they moved quietly toward the exit. "But, I'll take a gander and say it refers to a light or darkness that is in all of us?"

"Yes."

"Recognition of the wrong that you're doing to another person or even yourself isn't always clear until the deed is done. Would you agree?"

"Absolutely."

"I'm not a churchgoer or even especially devout. Semi-consciously, I think I choose the dove and all it represents, even though I also believe that when it comes down to it, I have no choice; it's almost innate," she continued in a hushed tone. "You might argue then, how much easier it seems to be to give into temptation than to resist it, and I would say it all depends on whether you listen to your conscience before its voice reaches a fevered pitch. The gentle whispers come from the light and the urgent rationalisations from the dark." Again, her eyes widened at her own words as she looked down at their still intertwined hands. Never before had she spoken this way to anyone. The evening had turned into a series of revelations. She felt disturbed and a sense of peace at the same time. "As for whereby I actually inherited that trait, I shall leave that to you, Mr. Novice-theologian, to work out." She smiled widely when she gazed up again.

He pushed the door outward. "A more than satisfactory answer," he said, his voice soft and husky. "Now, I definitely intend to walk you to your car and kiss you goodnight. It's the one intention I've had from the beginning."

Drove Incoming

†

P ROMISING HIM THE first knowledge of discovery (before any other organization), Paisley prevailed upon Dr. Everett Brandt of BIAI the opportunity to contribute to the dig efforts at the Gwellen site. He was also offered his choice of artifacts—for the Institute's private museum collection—after LEMM's picks, of course. However, a man like Dr. Brandt was not one to be sold on so-so prospects. To cinch the deal, since he was the best hero for the situation (regardless that there was no other alternative) Paisley hinted at a "tremendous" outcome and Everett had kindly chosen to accept assurance by her word alone.

A week later, she and Mallory both breathed a sigh of relief when Dr. Brandt's team arrived, as this solution effectively slashed the previous dilemma of how any progress would be made on the rest of the site when the entire workforce consisted of just three individuals. Yet, maintaining control of *their* project when the majority of the people on the site going forward were not *their* people, still worried the anthropologists, especially Mallory.

Not long after Dr. Brandt's staff actually started working, however, Paisley and Mallory's anxieties on this front whittled away. Ironically, when Mallory recalled the average workday before—the incessant questions and numerous other disruptions that five students caused—she could only marvel at the noticeable peace that came after the arrival of twenty-plus individuals.

There was no doubt he was an experienced and capable manager and his people were either well trained or well chosen. Perhaps it was his straightforward and authoritative but respectful nature that inspired a solid work ethic on the part of his employees. Granted, these laborers were not students; they were already skilled, and would be paid to do a very specific job. That said, it must have been a combination of factors.

Inquisitiveness and the jibber jabber of general awe, when faced with the fantastic reality of unearthing a several-ton rock, would have been natural, yet, no gossip or boasts outside of the confines of the dig site were heard. In fact, Dr. Brandt's employees were so professional and loyal that when a few members of the team were approached by Nigel in town, not only did they not hype up the work going on at the site, they reported the encounter to their superior.

Consequently, the following day Nigel pulled up the drive and before even reaching the dig site he'd been met and rebuffed by Everett at every turn. Dr. Brandt relayed the many, although intriguing, disruptive ploys Nigel used, trying to regain access. " 'Not *thee* Dr. Everett Brandt of *the* British Isles Anthropological Institute?' he asked. As you can imagine, I was quite nearly taken by the article added before my name. He also tried, 'I'm a doctoral student and I work here,' to which I replied it was peculiar we hadn't met before if that was truly his current status. Mr. Dupant explained, 'I was temporarily detained due to illness.' I informed him his services were no longer required. Persistent fellow, though. Next, he said, 'I'm sure Dr. Jacks wants to talk to me about you know who.' At this point, I could not help but laugh at the lofty sentiment. I do believe he took offense. By Jove an arrogant young man. He even resorted to, 'It's urgent I speak to my girlfriend.' I remarked, his ailment did not appear life threatening. While he stammered for another invention, I suggested he use his mobile *later,* or have a hospital ring for him, for that was the only emergency situation by which he was going to get through to speak with anyone other than myself. Suddenly, the *thee* didn't stand for much. He finally left in a disgruntled huff."

It was likely the extra hassles would continue. Regardless, it quickly became apparent what one influential person with resources could do for progress; and it was true, they did not need Nigel or any other student assistance now. Nearly a month further into the excavation, an acre of Mr. Fritchey's land continued to teem with the activity of two dozen workers in the twelve other subsites. They had made such great strides that Paisley would have to soon forewarn Everett to start being more watchful of both his team and for the contents of the pits.

Meanwhile, Mallory proceeded with her focus, trying in minor ways to maintain the secrecy of the current finds. For one, every evening she threw an ordinary tarp over Golly—any added serious obstacles to protect the area might well have been a beacon for prying eyes. However, hiding the skeleton wasn't the only precaution. She'd taken several pictures of the emblem found and afterward asked Grey to plaster over that area of the stone again with a layer of mud. Purposely hiding the symbols was definitely a measure on the shadier side of practice, but there was no other way of detracting attention from the spot. The stone in quadrant one was the only one unearthed in its entirety; even Mr. Fritchey could happen along.

She, Grey, and India advanced in their efforts, uncovering the rest of the giant's body. Every day they found themselves walking away from the site in a state of dazed confusion mingled with new excitement. So far, they had discovered that his skeleton was intact, an astounding fact in itself. The same carving on the surface of the stone was also embedded into his left temple and the back of his skull was elongated in almost an alien-like fashion.

Apart from the two factors: his sheer size and the extra bulbous skull, the specimen, known as Goliath, was definitely human but could not be classified further. There were several cultures that practiced head binding, which could possibly account for the head shape. Furthermore, a couple of other regions across the globe had uncovered unusually large skeletal remains. However, there was no one solid explanation for both factors present, least of all, in one artifact. Furthermore, the practice of head binding had not occurred historically in the British Isles, nor were any of the previously unearthed large skeletons quite as large as Golly.

It would not be possible to extract the giant from his grave for another few weeks, maybe months. The sedimentary rock surrounding him was compact and as hard and brittle as old cement; the lines of separation were distinct but the earth's hold on the body was steadfast.

Mallory and Paisley conducted countless hours of research through the archaeological databases for species specifications for either of the two defining factors—anything they could find that they could investigate further. Mere connections of straw could be made between Golly and the bones found in French caves in the early part of the nineteenth century. The data on these findings was sparse and what information was accessible told of figures under ten feet tall. Thus, every night they arrived at the same impasse: Until bone itself could be tested, there would be no leads.

In passing, on the night of the last finding—the abnormally large calvarium—Mallory expressed her trepidation to Grey, having grown to completely trust him as a colleague and respect him as such, as well. Oddly enough, without saying much, he continued to inspire a thoughtfulness that sometimes surprised her—similar to how freely she engaged herself in the interview on their first date.

India had proven herself to be trustworthy also, but she lacked the capacity of insight that only experience could bring. Thus, Mallory would not have told her that Golly scared her a smidgeon; in a way that a sense of something evil can give a person the heebie-jeebies without the person knowing why. This is exactly what she relayed to Grey.

His response was perplexing, if not oddly dramatic for him. He first asked her if she was shocked or truly scared. When she replied it was probably the former, he told her nervously that it was just anticipation she was feeling. His face looked almost inanimate, although his eyes took on a translucent quality. The green coloring of his irises seemed to recede until the tiny creases surrounding the pupils could be seen clearly. He abruptly embraced her, cradling her as though to keep her safe, while continuing to soothe her worries with cajoling words. He said that what she felt was only uneasiness with something seemingly unfamiliar to anything she'd ever encountered before. "Professionally," he said unnecessarily and almost as an afterthought. All the while, the tone of his voice sounded as though he was trying to persuade himself too. Finally, he added that she should remain on guard and trust her instincts. If she reached a point when she wanted to re-bury Goliath, he would support her decision and help with a shovel or bulldozer.

The next day, Mallory excused herself from working on Golly and spent her time visiting each of the other pits and going over the semiology of the carving on the stone with Paisley. Although she hadn't spent as much time considering it as she had the remains of the giant, the etching was puzzling as well. The stone itself looked as disproportionate as any other handcrafted henge stone, but the artwork was precision crafted. There was no possible chance the carving could be graffiti or an elaborate hoax—the stone had been underground for, at least, several thousands of years.

Glimpse of Trouble

†

A COUPLE OF hours before what likely would have been another very long workday, feeling again an uncomfortable curdling in the pit of her stomach in Golly's presence, Mallory suggested to Grey that they find their escape early, order Chinese food, and if not cliché, eat it right out of the carton. For some reason, the idea of monosodium glutamate infused noodles seemed comforting to her.

Grey quickly complied by abandoning his efforts on the parapet. As he began preparing to leave the pit for the night, for the first time since they'd started dating, he offered they go to his place instead of hers.

Less than an hour later, as she looked around at the starkness of his apartment she came to understand what he meant by his comment on their first date—how she wouldn't be able to glean anything meaningful about his life from bits and pieces.

The visible furnishings were purely functional: a dining table with one chair, a smallish sofa, coffee table, and a television set. In the adjoining kitchenette, there were but two dishes in the drying rack and a set of bowls and cups on a shelf above the sink. Aside from this, the only decorations were two black and white photographs—male relatives, presumably—

amidst the otherwise blank walls of the entryway. *So he is really, wow, really tidy.* Seemed like it, but she couldn't tell; with so few objects, nothing could be out of place.

While she slurped and chewed the noodles, she glued her eyes on Grey. She imagined every historian was like herself and Paisley; where for them, a collection of all manner of junk was considered an inspirational montage of sorts, if not art. Distinctly recalling her dormitory rooms in college and subsequent apartments she'd lived in with others, she could not recall one of her past roommates *not* having the same penchant to display *stuff*.

Marveling at how a person could live in such a place, devoid of personality for sixteen odd years, she blurted the question: "Grey, you have a crazy obsession room, right? Tell me you do, please." From her seat on the sofa, she pointed a chopstick down the shallow hall with three doors.

"Sorry to disappoint … I don't."

Mallory was taken aback by the blunt statement in that it brought forth the reality of a change occurring within her. She *was* disappointed and not because he wouldn't reveal a mental instability simply hidden behind a closed door. It was that he couldn't ease her mind. Confusing as this sounds, if he had revealed himself to be a nut job, she might feel validated in not having known. On the other hand, her chagrin stemmed from the fact that she was growing quite attached and to a relative stranger, no less.

Her mind spun out of control, another foreign occurrence when it came to romance. How could this have happened to me?—she wondered. He would be a colleague, at best, were it not for the physical connection between them when they touched or the relative easiness of their company. Perhaps he *had* used reverse psychology on her. *Was he one of those weirdos who moulded himself for his obsession—changing himself for me? Is that what he meant when he said he liked me just the way I am?*

Ironically, if he was being her ideal, despite him having answered all of her general questions, Mallory still did not feel she knew him. She could have just as well learned with a background check that he had two siblings, sisters named Aberdeen and Martine. They and his parents currently lived abroad in New Zealand where they'd moved when Grey was eighteen and away at college. After which, he lived in Queenstown for a couple of years before returning to Cornwall. She also knew he'd grown up in Portholland.

Setting her meal on the table, she shook her head. "I have to say, your place freaks me out a bit. How do you remain sane in an enclosed white box? This is a duplex? Who lives downstairs?"

Grey laughed, finally comprehending her bewilderment. "This was my parents' house. A while back, I converted the upstairs for my use, but hardly ever use it. I live downstairs mainly."

"Thank God!" Much relieved, she began eating again. She took another look around and with a mouth full, asked, "Why are we here if this is not where you live-live?"

"Downstairs is more impressive; I was going for cozy over leaving you with the masquerade of effects that belongs to my parents more so than me. Seems I've given you the wrong impression, regardless."

"This is your home now, though. Why do you keep their things if you don't want them? Surely, they can't expect you to hold on to their castoffs forever. Or why can't you move their stuff up here instead?"

"Although it's not really done up to my taste, it feels like home, even though they aren't here if that makes any more sense. I admit, I thought and hoped this apartment would be kind of a blank slate so you could form an opinion without first seeing me as just a grown man living in his parents' house."

"Grey, ehm, you're not a grown man living *with* your parents, though. Besides, how is your situation different from mine exactly? And do you judge me on that same basis?"

"There *is* a difference. My parents are living. Your house is a tribute to the memory of yours in a way and no one could fault you for keeping it … living in it just the way it is, so no, I don't, not at all. Consider it twisted logic. Also, my parents' choice of home decor is *different*. The main level requires explanation." He looked down into the carton and extracted a single noodle, holding it up for their mutual assessment.

"All right, I can accept that," she said. She nudged the half-full container on the coffee table. "Finish off the beef and broccoli. And here, I've more left of this than I can finish." Precariously holding out chopsticks laden with chow mein, she shoveled food into the empty carton he held. "To put it bluntly, a 'blank slate,' or an empty apartment just perpetuates the half-baked impression I do have. Apart from a few facts, I know nothing, really, about you. Shall I illustrate how little I know or knew as of ten minutes ago? Then maybe you can tell me if that's the way you want us to keep going. Still, I stand by what

I said before. I can't promise you anything." *Why do I keep saying that—especially since I'm the one pushing?* She scowled; she was further gone than he was, she was sure.

He nodded before tipping his head back to take a swig of beer.

"You have two sisters and the same number of dishes in your dish rack. Of course, there's no correlation, just the obvious facts, as I said. But, I'll assume you and your siblings do not dine in this otherwise practically empty hole when they come all the way from New Zealand to visit. Besides, only one of them could sit at the dining table. But, oh, wait, with you included, that still makes three people vying for one chair and two plates." She chewed on one side of her mouth, orchestrating a thin-lipped, concern-ridden look by furrowing her eyebrows with the other half of her face. "Dysfunctional family, yours—not unlike everyone's, I guess."

He laughed at the inanity of her assumptions.

"Unless you want me to assume that your guests, be it, family or friends come one at a time and you never invite more than one person to dinner. On the off-chance a third wheel happens along, perhaps he or she sits on the sofa and snacks out of his or her hand. Let's go back to your sisters since at least I *know* their names. You're lucky, let's say Aberdeen prefers not to sit while eating anyway. Can I call her Abby? Maybe it's Martine who prefers to dine in front of the television. Would I be remiss if I called her Marty?" Mallory rambled enthusiastically. "I could be entirely wrong. Reality is you still have standing-room only parties like back in your uni days. At these wild shindigs, no-name friends bring their own disposable cups to swig their ale as they, as well, eat *whatever* out of paper or plastic cartons. As I've only just been invited into your distraction-less sanctuary here, I conclude guests who eat takeaway is a prerequisite, a rule of thumb. But, really who am I to tell you it's strange to only entertain the company of those who bring their own dinnerware?" She raised the paper container to illustrate. "A word of advice, dining over candlelight might go a way toward making your flat *seem* more intimate. Girls like that, you know? It's possible you could have avoided my assessment altogether had *we* done that."

His eyes twinkled with mirth. "Next time we'll just have dinner in my *real,* humble abode."

"Brilliant plan. Personally, I might be less likely to take you up on that offer if I thought you were taking me home to meet your mother; good thing your mother isn't home, but someone else may not be as selective. Different strokes …" she said, grinning. Her voice trailed off, followed by a lull of silence; Grey's facial expression suddenly looked serious, although he was staring at her intently. *Have I again said something off-putting?* "Should we continue this little game … you're a semiologist, but not fluent in hieroglyphics; taught for four years, four years ago; you were born in—"

"I guess now is as good a time as any to start on that life story."

"That'd be downright lovely. I'll cross my fingers and hope you throw in a couple of 'I think's in there, not just stats and facts."

His face paled, he was obviously going to find the tale hard to tell. "But first, do you trust me? I need you to and I also need you to not be scared," he added, earnestly.

She tilted her head to the side and smiled, sheepishly. "I've spent the last two months unearthing a very alien, human giant; I'll try to contain my fright."

He searched her face for reassurance.

"Grey, I can take it if you *were* a member of a notorious band of miscreants. So long as you're reformed," she chided playfully, wagging a finger.

The Grey Line

†

WELL, I'LL JUST skip ahead of my birth and everything in between that day and six years later when I learned how to ride a bike. No, I'll skip ahead later." He was obviously nervous, the first couple of sentences out and he was already confusing the storyline. "So … Aberdeen was born first. She's four years older than me, and she hates being called Abby. Martine doesn't mind one way or the other—being called Marty. Everyone in the family calls her Martine because she chooses to live up to just Marty."

"How much younger than you is Martine?" she asked. She wasn't sure what Grey meant by his sister living up to the shortened version of her name, but Mallory was hoping to find out.

"Three years."

"And were you all … Are you close to them?"

"Aberdeen was always rather maternal. When I was little she dried my tears when I got hurt, fixed me up when I scraped a knee, as I became older she told me who I could and could not date, and stayed up late to make sure I made it home before curfew. Because of those kinds of dynamics, we are close but not friends. Martine, on the other hand, is capricious. I think it's because Aberdeen didn't play as big of a role in her upbringing. My parents were both working and away from home too much to notice when she started to waver. But she's a good girl. Martine. Sweet as you can imagine. She just concerns herself too much with other people's worries, taking little care of herself. She's been arrested twice, accepting the blame for the stupid actions of her friends. She's thirty-five, which means that's who she is for the long haul going forward.

"Full speed ahead now; when I was seven, my great grandfather, the man in the photograph on the left over there …" He pointed at the entryway, pausing thoughtfully. "Took me to a church of some kind, rather a temple. In the centre of a great hall inside this building was a Grecian style sculpture of a man standing on a roundish platform of carved earth. Behind him, independent of his body was a set of enormous wings, but they were proportionate to the figure. The wings were suspended from the ceiling by a heavy metal rod protruding from a cloud shaped stone."

"Wow, it sounds amazing, the symbolism alone … who was he meant to represent?"

"Alexiel, an archangel, and one among the Fallen," he said slowly, looking surreptitiously at her to gauge her reaction. Had she realized yet, what he just described?

"Ehm, you were seven?"

Apparently, she had not made the connection. "Yes, after that my grandfather took me to several locations with similar monuments … wings tethered to a representation of firmament and an angel-man standing on the earthly ground." Grey took a momentous pause, inhaling purposefully, slowly brushing his fingers through his hair. "In my family, it's been long believed that we males are descendants of the Nephilim—

the children the fallen angels had with human females. That is to say, Nephilim were not angels; they were flesh and blood." The words rushed out.

"You're telling me you're some kind of freak? A cultist?" she questioned, her eyes wide with astonishment. "Might not you have mentioned that before? Or was I supposed to infer?"

"No, I absolutely am not. Actually, I've spent my whole adult life trying to rationalise the strange occult ideas I was introduced to from an early age." He moved closer to her and she edged away cautiously.

"What are you not—a practicing heretic, an amateur in that vein, or some variation in between? I don't get it," she asked, grimacing and remembering the question he'd asked her on their first date about following the dove or the raven. "For that matter, if you have to prove it to yourself by knowledge over belief then you're in trouble, and I'm sorry but I can't and won't help." Her tone was unaccepting and she shook her head. This was a conversation she didn't want to have. *To each their own*, she thought.

"Mallory, please don't judge me, at least not until you've heard my story. I cannot help how I was raised and as far back as I go I've not found one member of my family who proclaimed him or herself as a black artist, per se. Way back when, a few of my ancestors practiced paganism and even possibly dabbled in witchcraft, but you'd be hard-pressed to not find the same in your own family if you go back far enough."

When she remained quiet, still leaning back onto the armrest at the far end of the sofa, staring at the empty carton on the coffee table—as though aware of a rodent scampering across the room—he nervously tapped and nudged at the container. Then absentmindedly he picked it up only to move it few inches toward the corner. She looked up, but her wary and mildly disgusted gaze transferred to him. Turning away, avoiding that expression, he continued with his explanation. His voice was low and bookish. "After Eden, God sent angels in human form to watch over people. 'Sentinels' they were called by one name, and 'watchers' is another. However, some of these angels began to lust after human females, and more than that, they maybe chose to leave their heavenly Estate in order to mate with them. The children, which resulted were the Nephilim, coming from the word 'nephal.' And God then cast those fathering angels out of Heaven permanently.

"There is some difference of opinion as to what 'fallen' means. In Hebrew, it just means 'to fall' or 'cast down.' Some ecclesiastics say the angels descended from Heaven because they chose to, and after the fact, they were barred from returning as a consequence. There are others who say, they fell from grace and were consequently dubbed 'Fallen Angels' by the human interpretation of the event.

"While they were all lumped together, there were definitely leaders and followers in the group. Some angels sinned against God in a multitude of ways, wanting actual power over others and men that they did not have in heaven or as mere watchers."

"Are you planning on getting to the part where I *should* base a judgement?" she asked him pointedly. "Because while this is all very interesting, if you're *not* a zealot, I don't know how this is relevant to you."

Grey stood silently and began to unbutton his shirt. She stared at him in bewilderment. Then he pulled the black t-shirt over his head and gazed down at her, expectantly. Slowly he turned. Across his broad back were what looked like two dark blue stains, one on either shoulder blade. The outer edges of the blotches fanned out and faded unlike any tattoo she'd ever seen—just like watered down ink seeping through fabric. Yet, the beautiful wings were nearly symmetrical to one another and the inner edge was darker, framing the bare skin along his spine; this center forming in the distinct shape of a man.

"So, you'd seen the carving on the stone before," she remarked.

Taking his time, he put his two shirts back on before turning to face her. The color and depth of his eyes appeared flat and the expression of his mouth was somber as well.

"But you seemed almost frightened when you saw it, if so, then why would you get a tattoo of it? Or maybe, it was the shock of seeing it on the stone that scared you since you didn't always 'rationalise the darkness' as you do now?"

"I've seen a huge variety of imagery related to the Nephilim. However, the wings with the cut out of the man have not once been among them. Search any of the databases and you won't find anything even close to it in one combined image. Photographs of the temple figures are not in any book either."

"Oh! The sculptures ..." Finally, it seemed she'd made the connection.

"Mm-hm, so while I said I grew up having knowledge of them, I had never before found actual evidence of their existence. I wouldn't say it was the carving that scared me. That fear rose to the surface when we started uncovering more of Golly. The carving was that much more frightening because it became personal suddenly."

"All right, I'm still confused. What you're saying is … that, ehm,"—she twirled a finger in the air—"on your back, came first. Well, not first, but you'd invented it and saw it later on the stone and Golly's temporal bone. You must have seen it and subliminally stored it away."

"Yes, and no. I'm not doing a very good job of making myself clear, even though I've run through this conversation in my head a dozen times. I was born with this. It's not a tattoo. Every male member of my family has it or has had the same mark, except it varies in size and location. Mine is the largest."

Mallory's eyes widened, not only in surprise. "So, you're a descendant of an angel … having said it out loud, I think that's possibly the strangest thing I have *ever* said … and we know what the giant in the pit is, part angel, part human—all right, now, maybe that statement takes the cake."

"Well, again I should clarify. An angel is a being composed wholly of spiritual matter, that isn't really *matter* in a chemical compound sense. We are therefore descended from the bodily form of them. Just as human bodies are shells for souls, when the watchers descended, their spirits were embodied. … In other words, the Nephilim *were,* and my family *is* zero-part angel. Golly is just bones now but he was flesh and blood once, like me, with a soul that God gave all humans. I think. However, spiritual beings and souls are not synonymous."

"I understand, but you do realise I have to tell Paisley …

about Golly."

"Mallory, I don't—"

"I assume you don't want to be tied to this … him in this context." She stared at the pads of her fingertips, methodically stroking them as she spoke. "Blimey, I don't even know how I would go about explaining any of it, anyway. As to that, how would I know what I know if not for you? And what if Everett finds another one—another skeleton and symbol? It doesn't make a difference, though. Science is science; we just have to leave religion out of it somehow. Otherwise, this could get crazy. People have found religious objects and iconography before, but they were artifacts of the civilizations. Prehistoric man existed alongside the dinosaur, who knew? It's going to get barmy, regardless."

"Mallory."

"Huh?"

"What about me?"

"What *about* you? I just said, I wouldn't tell anyone about your background or birthmark. You're just a man. That's what you said."

"All right, let me rephrase. What about us?"

"Ehm, I don't know that this changes anything between us. I understand why you were freaked out and you're right, I can't really blame you for how you were brought up. Overreacting to the topic of religion is a symptom of my profession. I apologize for that. You're not a creepy person and that's what matters now. What else is there?"

Eyeing her hopefully, scooting closer, and taking hold of her hand, he said, "My grandfather suggested I was some kind of key. It was prophesied by my great-great-great-uncle that a boy would be born with a magnified mark, where the wings would seem to diminish and the figure would be more pronounced."

She felt an odd sensation on her palm—not quite trembles—more like a vibration emanating from his. Pulling her hand away, she scratched it. "Did you feel that?"

"That's the first time you noticed? I felt it two years ago when I helped you up the pit ladder."

"Hm. What did he mean 'key'?"

"Right now, although the fallen angels no longer exist in bodily form, they do reside in a spiritual realm parallel with Earth. Before the time of judgement comes, the spirits of those angels are to descend to Hell for all eternity. This much is doctrine. However, there is no scriptural text that addresses what will become of the human souls of the Nephilim and that of *their* offspring when the Rapture occurs for the rest of mankind. After all, these children were completely human and played no conscious part in the original sin, yet, they may be guilty by the same original association.

"Although to a lesser profound extent than how Jesus's life and crucifixion absolved mankind of sin, it's been said that a man—born of these *different* genetics—will come out of the darkness and into the light. His life and death will represent a token of forgiveness from God for those human men who are and were burdened with the sin of their forefathers, as well as the fallen angels, too."

"Let me get this straight; now you're telling me that you're the sacrificial goat. And, correct me if I'm wrong, you're implying doomsday for all mankind happens within *your* lifetime. Since you are human with a human lifespan, within the next half-century is to be the end of all of us?"

"That's about the gist of it. No one probably cares about the Nephilim, their children, and their children's children except for those of us who were lead to believe we *are* their far-removed progeny. I assume I have a soul and feel in my being that I have one. Still, I'd like to take comfort in knowing I won't be punished for simply existing. I want to believe my family won't be, as well, for being what they can't help being."

She started chuckling and found she couldn't stop. Hysterically, she waved her hands in front of her. "I just thought ... I just thought, *how the heck* ... let's just chalk it up to hallucinogenic noodles," she said in gasps. "It's all a bit much, for a mere, normal mortal to take in. So, we'll just pretend this entire conversation never happened."

"What?"

"Tomorrow we carry on, as usual, making efforts to solve the mystery of Golly as we would any other archaeological find, through research. Eh? What do you say? I mean if the end of the world is coming, then what does it matter anyway? When it comes to it, I'll just classify him as Homo habilis gigantopithecus."

"Do you believe me or is it just that, as you said, too much to take in?"

"I believe you, kind of hard to cast aside the evidence. I can't un-see it." She gingerly stroked his back.

"I just want to make sure you don't think I'm barmy ... that I haven't scared you away. Because there is something between us, you can't un-feel either. Unless you didn't notice—the energy when we … ?"

"Oh! I would definitely say there is a supernatural quality about that too, although your shudders when I caressed your back now make more sense. I just thought you were sensitive there."

"You quiver when I touch the sides of your ribcage just under your breasts, ever so lightly. Maybe you would describe it the same way … the sensation is an equal blend of pleasure and torment."

She nodded.

"But, while together we are inexplicably electrifying, our connection is very real. I mean, there is nothing supernatural about me. In everything I've said, I didn't mean to imply I am anything but human. I promise, I do not have some magical ability hidden up my sleeve because of my birthmark, as it were."

"What a strange thing to say; magical powers never entered my mind. But, what do you call that tingling when we touch? For me it's very faint, just a whisper I wasn't fully aware of until now."

"I call it soul-mating, spiritual but non-magical, except in the poetic sense."

Instantaneously she pulled back.

Her defensive move away from him prompted Grey to say, "I hoped you wouldn't be scared of me and what I had to say. I'm so very glad you are not, but that you should be afraid of my choice of two words, frankly, is as unnerving as it would have been had you screamed at me in fear." He cupped her shoulders and pulled her closer. "Mallory, we have a connection. You can't deny it. Something deep within each of us recognises the other. That's all."

Again, she nodded, this time guiltily.

"Before this conversation is behind us, I should add that I was literally shocked when I touched the carving on the henge stone. It sent an almost painful jolt through me or so it seemed. I'm not sure it wasn't self-induced shock, however—as though I'd given myself a heart attack."

Mallory was still reeling from what they'd discussed this evening, especially Grey's later comments. She tried to dismiss the strange possibility of some grander meaning behind Grey's experience with the stone emblem. "Since you're not a witch, or, ehm, a warlock, that's probably what happened. I can only imagine the fright … you having spent your whole life steeped in this story."

By Jove

†

D R. BRANDT PEERED down into the pit, Paisley at his side. "Prepare yourself to be awed, Everett. Once you see what's under the tarp you'll understand."

"The site looks textbook otherwise. No other paraphernalia found? I look forward to seeing this object, but before I do, any details you can give me to prepare myself?" he asked. "By Jove, I am enjoying the anticipation."

"Just, scraps. Pieces of metal, broken pottery, that sort of thing," Paisley answered succinctly.

"The earth was remarkably clean and the level of this find in strata, puts the specimen at around the prehistoric times, but we know stone circles were being created no earlier than around four thousand years ago. My theory is that for some reason, holes were dug and the stones placed into those pits. This is the only explanation of why the two main artefacts in this trench are from vastly different times. What's stranger still is that when the hole was dug and the stones submerged, they just happened to miss the artefact under that canvas by a metre or so." As she explained, Mallory kept her eyes focused on Paisley. Grey was standing inconspicuously toward the outer edge of the pit, holding a tool in each hand. India was gazing up at the doctors, waiting for some cue as to what to do.

"I'm ready to be amazed," Everett announced.

Paisley descended the ladder first, followed by Mallory and then Everett. Once in the trench, they surrounded the covered artifact. Mallory nodded and gestured, "India, if you would do the honours." The student came forward to un-stake the corners while Paisley yanked out the ones closest to her at the head of the relic. The student rolled the tarp toward Dr. Bourne, slowly revealing Golly's tarsals, then his ankle bones, tibia and fibula, and so forth.

"By Jove!" The exclamation was followed by a loud, surprised guffaw. "This is indeed tremendous!" He walked around the carcass several times in amazed silence. A moment later when his obvious excitement was better restrained by professional skepticism, he added, "This must be some kind of elaborate deception."

"If it is, then a very clever one to have planted him here so carefully. To reiterate, the sediment is appropriate for this stratum; there's no way to reproduce it so meticulously," Mallory said solemnly. "And, just behind the ear, we've uncovered a small amount of membranous remains. Of course, we don't know if it is actually our corpse's tissue; my feel is that a trickster wouldn't have added that."

Everett crouched at Golly's feet and crawled along the length of his body. "Definitely real bone … but I'm stumped. This is absolutely unbelievable. Truly, truly astounding."

"He's been dubbed Goliath; we call him Golly," Paisley said.

"The size of his skull would seem to indicate he came *before* Homo neanderthalensis," Mallory suggested.

"But if our man Goliath was found by accident, just

happening to be near this particular megalith, then I would think we need to trench out the entire area within the circle, if not a little outside the perimeter."

Paisley turned her head quickly toward her peers. Her eyes widened at the prospect, probably of the added expense of it.

Everett continued. "The probability we shall find another specimen at the base of another stone just like this one is slender. The other pits could be empty. If we don't broaden the search we might miss something by assuming whatever we find will be situated exactly like Goliath, here."

"I agree. At first, I thought this was a burial site and imagined the stone was a headstone. Golly was positioned lengthwise almost exactly in line with the stone, it seemed to make sense and I've been pitching it all along. Now, I have a different theory, as I said, mainly because of what we know about the timeline … no other hengiform is nearly as old," Mallory offered.

"That's not to say the henge can't be the same age as Golly. It would surely have been easier for men of his size to fashion these types of megalithic structures," Paisley added.

"That is a definite possibility. Just because we've never found a circle older than four thousand years doesn't mean this one couldn't be the first," Mallory said. "Since the dawn of archaeology, there've been plenty of firsts."

"You're still the lead on this, Dr. Bourne, but I'd like to completely re-grid the site, furthermore, have a forensic team come out here and re-scan the acreage."

"We can discuss that later." In a much lower tone, Paisley

added, "A possible expansion of the excavation is currently not feasible, Everett. For one, I would have to account for the added costs with the LEMM board, let alone find that capital somewhere."

"No need to concern yourself, my dear," he said as quietly. "I shall incorporate it into my team budget and thus, BIAI will cover it as part of our agreement. I do have that authority, fortunately."

Striding over the few steps to stand before Mallory, Grey interjected, "If it's all right, I'll make our lunch run now." Pretending to brush away an imaginary lock of hair, he gestured with a pointed finger at his left temple. Simultaneously, Everett knit his eyebrows in consternation at the graduate student's back.

She smiled crookedly and nodded. "Mm, thanks, Grey. Bring me back a beef pasty from Govenek's." If her new theory separated the stone from the skeleton, then how would she explain the semiology on the stone was also reflected on the giant's temporal bone?

Once Grey departed, Everett replied, "I cannot recall being as disinterested in my own academics some twenty odd years ago. Even then I could hold off my appetite for more important things."

"Yes, but we've been staring at Golly's mug for a while now, Dr. Brandt. However, after a time, the stomach remembers when it's getting near on normal lunchtime," Mallory said calculatingly.

"I suppose so. As we were discussing, I don't know if I would go as far as to classify a new species of hominid just yet, he could be just an anomaly, a mutant. If we find no others like him then … what's this?" he asked, drawing an air circle around the concerning area of Golly's skull.

"That's another story for another day. There are too many characteristics that we have little explanation for at the moment. We'll talk about it again when we have more to go on beyond speculation. I'm sure you'd like to resume your work and Mallory should get back to hers," Paisley said.

"Most definitely," he said. "I appreciate your having shown me. Can I take steps to organise that reevaluation of the site I proposed?"

"Yes, but still we're to keep this all under wraps. Actually, that matter has become a bit of a problem. I have half a mind to get Keaton over here and have him write up a story to debunk what Nigel started to perpetuate. Only, I can't think of anything believable and at the same time absurd enough, except to confirm the tale that we did, in fact, find an ape. Somehow, people will view it as an even more irresistible spectacle, one that they have to see for themselves; I'm certain of it."

"Alternatively, you could consider extracting Goliath expediently from this pit so the henge stone alone can be availed to public view. This would appease the curious, in general, and we wouldn't have to continue with the current measures that prevent visitors entirely. Otherwise, once the larger excavation phase gets underway, we shall have to hire a few official guards. My team and I won't be able to play watchdog then. I've had to turn Mr. Fritchey away a few times, Nigel twice, and the second time he brought others with him."

"A distraction; there's an idea … although we shouldn't

really rush Golly's excavation. Let's give it a few weeks and see how far we get," Mallory suggested.

Everett looked back at the giant skeleton one more time before leaving the pit with Paisley. Mallory sauntered to the other side of the stone and retrieved a canvas stool. Unfolding it at the base of Golly's feet, she sat and watched India for a minute. The student had again diligently begun the painstaking process of picking away at the stony sediment between his ribs. "India, cover him and let's talk. Grab that stool while you are at it."

"All right." Depositing the tools in the bucket at her side, she casually draped the tarpaulin over the remains. "Have I done something wrong, Dr. Jacks?"

"Not that I can tell, but I don't really know. I'll just open by saying the details are none of my business, so you don't have to tell me those. However, a completely truthful yes or no will suffice. In other words, I'd like there to be no vagueness in your answer. A while back, Dr. Brandt said Nigel came by asking to see his girlfriend."

India shook her head as she looked down at her hands, but didn't interrupt.

"I think we all assumed that Nigel was lying. Partly that was because of what you said when you returned to the project. You implied he'd lost favour with you. He might have done at the time, however, he came back and repeated the same excuse. As you heard, this time with others around. Now, it makes no difference to me whether he and you are in a relationship, insofar as it being a personal thing, but if he wasn't lying ... well then, I'd have to ask you to leave this excavation.

I like you, India, but we've also gotten into the habit of speaking frankly around you. If I could trust you, that wouldn't be a problem. If I can't, though … you see what I'm getting at?"

"This is more important to me, Dr. Jacks … this project." A desperate twang pitched India's voice a touch higher than her normal cadence. "So, yes, you can trust me and I never speak to anyone outside of here about it. I swear to god! Nigel and I are *not* together. I am *not* his girlfriend, although that's not quite sunk in with him," she said vehemently. "Honestly, I think he doesn't know what he feels and he's just using my name and our previous relationship as an excuse for his daft—stupidity."

"I can't tell you how relieved I am to hear it. Although I said I didn't care one way or the other, for the record, you deserve someone better than Nigel anyway."

"Thanks. I could tell you didn't like him."

"He annoyed me, yes, and it perturbed me somewhat that he had an influence on you; I wouldn't say I *disliked* him. That would have required me to think about him more than I did and do. How old are you, India?"

"Twenty-three. I opted to skip the Master's level so this is my first year in the doctorate program."

"Very young."

"Yeah, but I've always known what I wanted. Rest assured Dr. Jacks, my goals do not include Nigel. He's still a boy."

Crossed Paths

†

1N THE TENT, they silently perused the new subfolder and master document Grey had uploaded to the project folder on the internal network. The account of the semiology on the stone, which included, the human figure, the backdrop stain of wings, and the eye emblazoned on the figure's chest was thorough. Each line item description referenced complimentary visual examples, which were attached separately. In turn, there were also spec sheets for the images, indicating where, when, and under what circumstances a particular graphic was found, what time period it was said to have been used, and from what civilization the symbol was originally derived.

The human figure, as represented in drawings, was seen as far back as thirty-thousand years ago in cave paintings found in France and Romania. Wings were depicted in art, mainly, when Christian-based iconography became popularized. The symbol of the eye was first seen in the ancient civilizations of Egypt, of which Grey had already informed them.

Mallory noticed he had not included examples of the disk that appeared under the etching's figure on the stone. They'd spoken about it and he surmised it would do more harm than good to cast attention to this detail. It was better to let people assume the shape represented a simple platform. However, he interpreted the shape as having the opposite of a divine connotation; essentially the reverse of a halo—still signifying a spiritual nature—and perhaps also a symbol of Earth, the habitation of man. A disk was often typically in hieroglyphics above the heads of rulers and had several supposed meanings.

"Grey has turned out to be quite an asset to this project," Paisley said. Shifting sideways in her chair, she added, "And is it just me, or is he more than that to you? I mean I know you two were dating, but Aly, you seem different."

"Paiz, I have no idea *what* he is." In all its vagueness, this statement was truthful. "I only know he's done something to me, I can't explain." Another fact was that Grey and Mallory's relationship with him had caused a rift between the lifetime friends. They had previously told each other everything and she had not mentioned to Paisley an inkling of what Grey had revealed privately about himself.

"And Keaton? Have you told *him* that?"

Mallory raised her head from her tablet's screen; there was a foreign edge in her friend's voice when she asked these questions. Her back had been to Paisley until this point. She twisted in her seat to respond. "I didn't realise I needed to tell your brother anything about who I'm dating and how it's going. I've never done so before. A long-ago snog hardly qualifies your brother to be the warden of my personal life." In a gentler tone, she added, "Apart from that less than platonic moment when I was sixteen, Keaton and I are no more than friends now. You know that. You should also already know I've not harboured any notions of us ever being otherwise, and at the same time, I can't be held responsible for anyone else's fancies.

Tell me you understand that and you're just sounding weird because you're being protective."

"I know … sorry. I am, I guess—feeling protective of both of you. I thought you two were inevitable. I guess I was wrong."

"You don't have to apologise, so long as you have no expectation that I'm going to retract what I just said. Because Keaton and I together as one is not a foregone conclusion in my mind, and I would think I would be the first to know, despite how obtuse I am sometimes," Mallory said, smiling.

Paisley returned the smile with a combination nod and shake. As pretty and intelligent as she was, Mallory was clueless when it came to reading the signs of attraction from the opposite sex. As far back ago as the flirtations from boys at school, when Paisley and she were but teenagers themselves, to the owner of Dredges Pub, who persisted to this day, her friend was oblivious of pubescent hopes then and remained so now.

"How about you and Everett?"

Paisley blushed. "We've reached an understanding, specifically that I've had a crush on him since uni. And while there couldn't have been an *us* when I was eighteen and he in his thirties, the age difference is now a moot point." She rose from her chair and walked over to the tent opening. Gazing over the site, she said, "It's madness to think that with everything I've done in my life, this one project has changed it all. It is the making of us … or will be."

"By Jove, it's uncanny," Mallory said, laughing at the phrase she'd come to connect with Everett.

"Ever notice how the more you're around people the more you pick up their habits, mannerisms, and even way of speaking?"

Mallory nodded and smirked in anticipation of what Paisley was going to say.

"Well, I've vowed to myself to let him keep that particular phrase for himself. It's so ridiculous but I find it incredibly cute." Changing the subject Paisley said thoughtfully, "The rains are coming." The tepid skies graded toward darker clouds in the distance. The light rain this time of the year had slowed the excavation progress. Within a few weeks, advancement on that front would come to a standstill. "Everett suggests we canopy the pits so we can keep working through the winter."

After the results of the subsurface scans, the topsoil overburden removal for the entire area, encompassing the henge, took place two weeks ago. Looking out, the site was a much larger muddy pit now. Needless to say, Mr. Fritchey's initial enthusiasm and support waned, along with it, his patience. No sooner had the bulldozers broke ground again then did he file a petition for the cessation of the project altogether, claiming extensive destruction was done to his property already. For three days, the equipment remained parked on the property and permission to proceed had been rescinded.

When Paisley received notification the project could resume, the farmer came by to express his fury personally, not having been apprised himself. He went away in a huff but as retaliation, he began to visit the site daily, sometimes taking his morning coffee just beyond the roped-off perimeter.

It was only yesterday that the town council clarified for

him that he had no choice but to accept the matter. The fact was, while the land was deeded in his name, he did not own it outright. First and foremost, the land belonged to the country and the government was its overseers. Bottom line was that preservation and investigation of history trumped personal land claims. Thus, this morning the doctors arrived onsite to see a table with four chairs and a large umbrella set up just outside of the section of the excavation site where Mallory, Grey, and India worked. They couldn't send Mr. Fritchey away. So instead, Mallory dismissed her assistants. She would spend the day in the tent with her partner until they could figure out how to continue to keep Golly a secret.

"That would also hinder prying eyes. In case I haven't mentioned this before … as a board member and excavation lead, I don't think I could go back to doing things the way we did them before Everett showed up, and with him his resources."

"I'm with you there and working on it. Everett and I are negotiating his having a more permanent role on future projects. I've considered enacting that role with this project, as a tester. What do you think?"

"He's proven himself trustworthy, I'd say. Not that there was really ever a question of his character—his reputation preceded him in that respect—but at least now we know he prefers teamwork over the usual competitive dynamics that exist among scientists vying for their piece of fame. It would be better to solidify that commitment, however, on both sides, so he's working *with* us instead of for us as well as himself."

"I'm so glad you agree. But, tell me honestly, do you think

that by going forward I'd be blurring the line between my personal relationship with him and our professional one? Because if he and I don't work out, then it could affect the business ... it has taken a long time and a good deal of hard work to get to where we (you and me) are today."

"Paiz, the different sides were always intertwined; you'd just be making it official. I think you're being overly cautious. He was mostly just your friend before this project; you'd not actually worked with him, except for in the advisory capacity as members of the LEMM board. Now you have a work connection, as well. So, regardless if anything personal changes, one core aspect of your relationship won't ever fail. You'll both still respect one another in the morning." Mallory grimaced, knowing full well what her friend was going through, in more ways than one. Despite the fact that both she and Paisley preferred casual relationships—and as mentioned, trysts were the norm—now, Grey was still an integral member of the crew, and there was Keaton.

Given Paisley's recent bouts of protectiveness, Mallory was even less likely to mention a similar dilemma she faced over twenty years ago. For the briefest of teenage, synaptic firings, she had had to decide whether her best friend would forgive her should a relationship with said brother end. Thus, for that reason and others, it never truly began. "I think it makes sense, but, I also have to admit I'm personally and professionally invested in Everett myself if that makes you feel any better. The aspect of my *job* that I disliked most was the staffing and subsequent supervising of our minions. Everett has relieved me of that responsibility and I've been able to go back to enjoying what I do. It doesn't feel like a job again. If there's to be a vote on his position, he has mine." Pouring herself another cup of coffee from the carafe on the camp stove, she rejoined Paisley at the tent opening. Blowing into the brew, the semi-burnt aroma wafted before her nose. "He doesn't have any farming stuff to do?" she questioned, eyeing the distant portly figure of Mr. Fritchey's with annoyance. "I didn't realise sheep and cows were left to fend for themselves in winter and it's not *even* winter. I want to be a farmer so I can sit on my arse for six months of the year."

"He'll either realise that he does have something better to do before or after he gets bored. Either way, I'll make sure to have your area covered as soon as possible."

"Look." Mallory nudged her head in the opposite direction. "What's Keaton doing here?"

The two tall figures of Keaton and Everett stood conversing. As though his ears prickled, the dark-haired, blue-eyed face of Paisley's brother turned to glance their way.

"I don't know." His sister waved and beckoned to him.

Man Friends

†

GOOD MORNING, INDY. Paiz." Keaton Bourne was as textbook attractive as they came. There was no denying that. He bore himself more as a gentleman than your typical journalist did. However, he was the opposite of stodgy; the crinkles around his blue eyes told plainly that he smiled often.

"What are you doing here?" Mallory asked directly. "And how did you persuade Dr. Brandt and his henchmen to allow you access into our little, rather large now, inner-sanctum of mud?"

Keaton didn't answer right away; instead, he sauntered past the women toward the coffee decanter on the burner. Dumping a creamer into the cup and stirring it into his coffee with a plastic spoon, he took his beverage and sat unceremoniously in his sister's uncomfortable office chair. His eyes grazed over the uninteresting contents of her makeshift desk, before pausing to study the laptop monitor situated in front of him. It displayed a screensaver image of Stonehenge illuminated only by the light of the stars and moon. "A modern pagan captured at the witching hour," he said, pointing at a tiny silhouette standing between two stones. Flipping the cover shut, he stood. Walking casually around the enclosure, he perused the rest of the tent with a casual eye while stopping periodically to peer into some of the boxes, which contained nondescript artifacts collected from throughout the site. "I've seen these somewhere before. Where? I wonder. Your's or Paisley's living room, no doubt," he said, grinning.

"Keaton?"

"Yes yes, sister dear. Believe it or not, I'm here because Fritchey called up the paper this morning and requested we cover the story. He argued it was about time and that while he couldn't boot you off his property, in turn, you couldn't do anything to prevent him exercising his right to market the spectacle. In an effort to recoup his loss, you see. He pled his case convincingly. The excavation could take years, he said, but it didn't mean people should be denied their glimpse of a national treasure, which just happened to be on his land. Just so you know, he wants to sell tickets afterward and no one can or will stop him."

"Ugh. You don't mean to really give people that glimpse, do you?"

"I most certainly do intend that, my girl-Indy." He grinned. "Everett mentioned a portion of all thirteen stones has been excavated. What say you give me basic dimensions and some generic history about henge and I can take it from there? And I'll be taking a few nondescript photographs, as well."

"Keaton, you sound suspicious. As if you know something, although I can't imagine how you could. I hope you haven't allowed Nigel's outrageous claim to befuddle your blockhead," Mallory said, squinting at him skeptically.

"Righto, you may cease being concerned. This noggin is selectively blurry, but airtight," he said, knocking on the crown of his head. "Paiz told me vaguely that you'd found something very important. I'm curious, as it is in the nature of a reporter to be, but my lack of burning need to know exactly *what* is also probably why I'm a failed journalist at that."

"Part of the plan was to have Keaton do a write up anyway," Paisley said. "Mr. Fritchey and the general public have no idea of the significance of the site other than the stones, so we might as well move forward and give them the boring same old story. We'll get some visitors and then soon it will be old news."

"News has that tendency," he muttered. "To get old. Speaking of which, who's this Grey McKnight fellow?" he asked, bending down to look into a random box.

"I'm going to go have a word with Everett." Grimacing, Paisley quickly exited the tent.

"Ehm, my … my boyfr— Well, dang it, Keaton. We're dating all right?"

"We are? You should have told me; I would have brought you a nosegay."

"I can't seem to say the word, sounds all wrong. I'm nearly forty for Pete's sake."

The raven-haired superhero let out a rumbling laugh. "That does not sound promising at all. Tell him I offer him my condolences."

"That's not what I meant. It's just so new. We haven't labelled it … I don't think."

"I'm sure, but then again, as I said new things have a way of getting old. It's the old things that hold value."

"Aren't you just a clever Trevor?"

"I have been accused of that more times than I can count, which makes me rather dumb actually, by my calculations."

Mallory struggled to get the words out; somehow, she knew Keaton needed to hear them. "Grey's my boyfriend; there, I've said it."

Suddenly Keaton's playful expression sobered as he assessed the handsome, giant figure standing in the doorway of the tent.

"That sounds … I don't know—wrong," Grey announced.

"That's what I said," she agreed.

"Mm, I haven't been a boy in a long, long time and if you exclude that prefix then 'friend' would be a highly inadequate way of describing my role, I'd argue." Smiling and approaching Keaton with an outstretched hand, he said, "Hello, Grey McKnight, also known as Dr. Jacks's assistant, underling, right-hand man, *lackey*."

"Keaton. Paisley's brother and Mallory's close *manfriend*." There was a definite challenge in the icy blue orbs, but he shook the boyfriend's hand anyway.

Grey's eyes narrowed and grew dark and his jaw tightened. Turning abruptly toward Mallory, his gaze automatically softened. "India and I were working with Dr. Brandt's team in quadrant twelve … You should come see when you have a chance." He nodded briefly at Keaton before turning to leave. She jumped to her feet to follow.

"Tell Paisley I'll need that tour," Keaton said dryly.

Containment

†

UADRANT TWELVE WAS just a sliver of the whole site situated 270 degrees due west and adjacent to Golly's location at 295 degrees northwest. Mallory had chosen this numbering strategy early on, beginning with the northernmost point of the parcel. From there, she counted clockwise and divided the circle into sensible parts based in the preliminary scans of the area. Thus, although Golly's residence was the first excavated, it was the last piece of the pie. Leaving the tent, she caught up with Grey a few paces outside of the structure, and together they walked toward the location of the new find.

"I guess I never thought to ask if *you* were previously attached," he muttered. "I assumed … since I hadn't seen you *with* anyone. Regardless, your friend seemed to not take it so well—that I'm your current 'manfriend.'" He grinned thinly and added, "Which leads me to think he may have made a few assumptions as well. Actually, there seem to be several people confused, myself included. Do I have competition I don't know about? It kind of felt like it."

"Keaton and I grew up together, but I guess there's always a bit of that between a man and woman. At least, that's what I've been told."

"Not if it's made clear. For example, India asked me to

dinner. I'm sure she wouldn't have if she knew about you and me, especially considering you're her work-study sponsor. I would think she respects you more than she wants to date me."

She unconsciously began to walk faster, keeping her gaze focused on a distant point on the horizon, although she only had a vague idea of what that actual visual spot was. The sky was misty, blurry, and gray. "How you choose to respond to India is your own affair," she replied shortly, gritting her teeth. More annoying than the tingling jealousy she felt was the surprise of the solution that instantaneously came to mind: dismissing her rival from the project. So much for the separation of work and play, *or* her inability to become emotionally attached.

"Mallory, stop for a minute. I don't really understand what the problem is. As far as I can tell I'm not being pushy; it's still up to you, but mutual respect is all I ask. Are you going to give me a little more than terse replies? Because I can't read your mind and our relationship will continue to be as confusing to others and ourselves as we make it."

"I simply want to maintain a level of professionalism while at work. Is that too much to ask? Although it may seem odd … that's hard to do if you were to call me Mallory, for example, and another student is expected to address me as Dr. Jacks— her superior. You'll notice I even call Everett, Dr. Brandt, for the most part, onsite. And when I remember, Paisley is Dr. Bourne. It's for the sake of that professionalism. But there's no question; they are still my friends. So, sorry, it's really not that complex as to be baffling." Her explanation sounded rational enough in her own ears. The beginning was all right.

"Yes, but, you'd be fine if I went out with India then,

huh?" he inquired, tilting his head downward in an attempt to meet her averted gaze. He redirected her face by crooking a finger underneath and giving her chin a gentle nudge. Green eyes sparkled with mirth; if he couldn't read her mind, somehow, he still gleaned that she was struggling with an extrinsic emotion.

"No, Grey, I would not be fine with it, but it's your choice to make," she said brusquely.

"You know I choose you."

"Then why does any of this make a difference?"

"Because there are other people in the world who would appreciate knowing that as well. Ironically, they can only know that if we know it ourselves."

She nodded, tucking her chin toward her neck in thought. Suddenly she raised her head and gazed deeply into his eyes, exposing herself to him in silence for a good long pause. He seemed to smile without moving his mouth. She wrapped her arms around his torso as a frightened child might do. Never in her life had she uttered the words to anyone but her mother and father; she hoped Grey heard them anyway. Feeling his lips grazing the top of her head she squeezed tighter before extracting herself from the circle of his arms.

For the remainder of the walk, a couple hundred feet, they held hands and observed the workers below diligently hauling away buckets of dirt. Even as they approached the location of the current interest, she could not see anything of the new spectacle. Drs. Brandt and Bourne were standing in front of it, blocking her view. The fact that other people were hovering around suggested the find wasn't one like Golly.

Mallory descended the ladder and proceeded toward the spot. Although the object was obscured amidst the dirt surrounding it and only a portion of it protruded from the ground, immediately she identified the snout and tooth of an unidentifiable creature.

"Prehistoric," Everett said. "Same sediment layer," he added, vaguely. "Which means, by Jove, that we can infer your time estimate is legitimate, Dr. Jacks. What we have here is quite phenomenal." Although still exciting for an archaeologist, uncovering dinosaur bones, in this day and age, would no longer have been uncommon. The significance of Dr. Brandt's remark lay in the dichotomy of these million-year-old, animal bones being found alongside a would-be much younger henge structure. Also, the peculiarities were adding up; Golly was looking more like a humanesque form of dinosaur with each passing day.

"Keaton's waiting in the tent. Maybe snapping photos of a couple of the stones in quadrants one and two will do, in other words, *before* we dig up anything else. Come to think of it, we're not going for a long-term show and tell. So, the farther away Mr. Fritchey's publicity stunt is from the areas we are working on, the lower is our chance of us becoming tour guides. Let's just decide here and now that those areas will also be the last excavated and keep them un-tented so people can get their gapes and awes until they become bored with it."

The others nodded in agreement. "Regardless, first priority will be getting the tents up over specified dig areas," Paisley said.

"And Grey, get someone to help you move Mr. Fritchey's

setup over there so we can resume work as soon as our canopy is installed."

Paisley and Grey left to do their parts while Mallory crouched down, gingerly and ineffectively brushing away debris from the nostril of the beast with a stray tool. "This guy's pretty far from the stone," she voiced ponderously. "Maybe it's right to assume the stone and the carcass are independent of one another, as well. Everett, Dr. Brandt ..." she corrected self-consciously, stopping to glance around for signs of India. "Everett, I have to say I feel rather sorry for the henge. The stones have not been getting much of our attention. We should try to determine if in fact they were dropped into pre-dug ditches."

"Come this way, I want to show you something," he said, motioning an outstretched hand toward the nearest henge stone, thirty or so feet away. The megalith in question was only partially excavated. The Northeast face was still covered in fifteen feet of earth. Everett's tall frame and a long arm reached up. With two fingers, he traced the vertical edge between stone and earth, pausing a few times at points in his demonstration where the dirt showed horizontal signs of a gradation from one sedimentary layer to another.

"The strata are intact ... making the entire site ... prehistoric," Mallory voiced in subdued awe. It would have been impossible not to disturb each stratum if a ditch was dug and the stone placed into it.

"It would seem so."

They stared at one another in bewildered excitement. Everett's brown eyes twinkled. "While everything, and I do mean everything, seems fantastical, the white elephant in the room, specifically in your quadrant must be a figment of our imaginations, surely. How will we ever discover the story to it all, Mallory? It's humbling, wouldn't you say? To be in the midst of such an extraordinary place as is this small circle."

All Mallory could do was bob her head in agreement. Casting a glance at the barely discernible dinosaur nose, she mentally ticked off the strangeness of the facts and shuddered. The same gnawing fear and uncertainty she still experienced around Golly momentarily replaced her excitement. Everett looked at her quixotically and she swallowed hard. "Definitely fear-inducing, in addition to being exciting," she muttered. "Mind if I help out here for the rest of the afternoon?"

"Of course, feel free. Your student is at number ten. I think you were looking for her earlier."

It was Mallory's turn to cast a questioning glance at him.

"From what I've observed, adoring glances and such, I believe she is falling in love with a certain man. I advise you nip that in the bud at your earliest convenience, my dear, if you care at all, for the man and her," Everett said, smiling crookedly. He shook is silver-haired head and sauntered away.

Well, dammit, she thought. She was no good at this sort of thing. A relationship was always a connection solely between two people—regardless of exclusivity—and it should be the task of the target to deal with his or her sniper. She didn't expect Grey to confront Keaton. So why did she have to lay her claim to Grey, as though she were a cavewoman with a club? She traipsed past the activity in the current area, dodging people, tools, markers, etcetera, and then through quadrant eleven. Spotting India seated in front of a grid next to the henge stone between this area and the next, she headed in that direction. The girl looked up and waited expectantly for Mallory to say something. Ten feet before she reached India, Grey came out of nowhere, swooped her into his arms, and planted a kiss firmly on her lips.

When he let her go, she said breathlessly, "I guess that takes care of that."

"Not that I didn't want to … sorry to have to bend the rule, Dr. Jacks." He grinned, tipping his forehead toward hers. "Premeditated, yes, but it had to be done for both our sakes, not to mention, hers," he said in a husky whisper.

"She just asked you to dinner, it wasn't like she proposed," Mallory said in an equally hushed tone. "You could have just said, 'no.'"

"Well, dinner was the first invitation and precursor; desert was mentioned once or twice," he whispered into her ear. "I just needed to get my point across sooner rather than later, so I kept it simple."

"Oh," she uttered. Approaching India again, she caught a glimpse of the girl's red face bent over her task. She turned back to Grey and asked, "Did you move Fritchey's setup?"

"All taken care of, and Dr. Bourne took the reporter to one and two for the photos, but not before she called to order the canopy for quadrant thirteen. It will be installed overnight and ready by morning."

"Did you hear that India? We can resume tomorrow," Mallory said when the student remained focused on the pile of rubble before her. "I would be happy if you re-joined us, but if you'd rather not …" she added tenderly.

Finally, looking from her sponsor to Grey, India bestowed them with a simpering smile and nodded, tucking her head toward her chin again shortly thereafter.

Blimey, this debacle had been brewing under my nose for who knew how long, Mallory pondered. She recalled India's comment about Nigel just being a boy and suddenly the lightbulb went off in her head. Beside her, she glanced wide-eyed at Grey; thankful he understood her without her having to speak, as well as for his ability to act before she'd even realized there was a problem—and despite her numerous discouraging comments.

Together they walked around the yard, examining each section of the site proper. Several regions of the grid were staked with short, colored posts—ranging from yellow to red, indicating particular care should be taken to not over-cut those plots. The red-marked areas were not to be handled by laymen diggers, at all.

How they could have even imagined at the onset they could excavate the site with one archaeologist and five students was now unfathomable; granted the scope of the project had expanded well beyond what the initial analysis indicated. Still, thirteen stones alone would have been difficult to manage given those same resources, especially as more than half of the people assets—students—had been relieved of their positions.

As mentioned previously, Mallory contributed very little to the budget considerations for projects, except for following Paisley's instructions on that front. In fact, she rarely thought about it. However, now she wondered, with their new partnership with Everett, which of their previous frugal ministrations could be tossed to the wayside and what new advancements they'd be adopting to practice. Perhaps they could even get a new coffee maker.

Everett was backed by the largest archaeological institute in all of Great Britain. They'd have access to better technology and testing equipment and larger groups of skilled workers, at the very least. As she and Grey continued to trudge through some muddy parts of the site, she thought that with LEMM's budgetary constraints, they would never have been able to pitch a tent over each subsite, for example. What was she thinking? Canopying *any* area of the parcel would have been an extravagance and, therefore, would not have come up for consideration.

An oblong rectangle in number seven, laying exactly perpendicular to the henge stone, looked suspiciously familiar, but it was marked with green pegs—signifying it was all right to remove sedimentary layers up to fifteen feet further. She would ask Everett to review the subsurface scans again. The fact that the zone was pegged, at all, meant the images had shown perhaps a trace of something there. Considering its placement and size, the section could be mismarked; she would rather it be treated with the same carefulness as a yellow tagged plot, just in case.

Multiplicity

†

1 T WAS SUMMER again, over a year since the Gwellen henge was first discovered. The second Homo habilis gigantopithecus was dubbed "Adam" by India. While Grey took exception to this name—as he knew the skeleton was a Nephilim, and therefore, not one of God's creations entirely—he couldn't voice his opinion to anyone but Mallory. Absurdly, this was the name he'd suggested for Golly, before fully realizing beyond his personal affiliations what the giant was. The third skeleton was named "Tiny" just because now it was near preposterous to consider a mutation having caused gigantism in three individuals and they all buried in the same general locale.

Adam was discovered in quadrant seven and Tiny in number three. Like Goliath in thirteen, each body was over fifteen feet long, wore an identical carving on the left temple, and was situated at the base of a henge stone with a matching etching depicted on it. Yet, these commonalities aside, there were certain expectations of communal burials that were *not* met.

It was customary for most civilizations to bury their dead with items of value, as either a token of another's esteem or as tools to guide or protect them in the afterlife. The entire area had been excavated, although the bodies themselves had not yet been extracted. No other artifacts were found in the vicinity. This was perplexing; anthropologists considered adding grave goods a common practice of ancient civilizations. Leaders, especially, were sent off with tributes, and these bodies—buried with such great effort—were definitely special. The dilemma in persisting with the preconception was that there were no human settlements during prehistoric times. One couldn't impose a later practice onto a much earlier lifestyle just because it was common.

Therefore, Mallory's theory that henge would also have been burial grounds was, at first, received by the anthropological community with deference. As one case study, it was just an unproven hypothesis; one she'd postulated before without the Gwellen site as proof. And, ironically, she suspected their current site was not an exception. If other henge were dug up, perhaps they would find carcasses there as well. Who was to say how many subterranean henge existed?

The team found the closed-minded perspectives of academia frustrating. There was always ready opposition and once an idea was finally won over, scientists were less likely to be swayed from their mindset. Would their peers have been ready to accept the possibility if they found Golly, Adam, or Tiny clutching at a twenty-four-karat gold scepter? Regardless, very few individuals would voice their support in the opposition of a once foregone conclusion. Mallory and Paisley were lucky to know of such a person and he was a partner at that. Dr. Brandt took it upon himself to pitch the case to BIAI and suddenly Mallory's papers were published in every respectable scientific journal. Funding practically came flying through the doors.

Not that she was particularly interested in bandying the issue again; Mallory could see from both sides, the situation was difficult. An anthropologist might speculate and make a claim—this is the reality of being a scientist in the first place—but the community would still need to be convinced. The acceptance process was long and arduous. However, if said anthropologist could obtain credible backing then that process would go much faster.

Her primary example revolved around the now famous but meager remains of a specimen named Sally. Within a year of her finding (possible with the right support), Sally came to represent an entirely new species of human, when there were, initially, many who disputed the claim. Drs. Bourne and Jacks were two of those early opposers. Although it was obvious Sally was a primate, the doctors believed her to be non-human. Her arms, legs, and pelvic bones were not that of a bipedal creature, that much could be ascertained. Somehow, this seemed only to support the appended claim: Sally was an example of the evolutionary branching off of apes and humans. Advocates further explained away the paleontology with speculations that early humans had not always walked upright the majority of the time. The issue became too convoluted in the evolution versus creationism debate that Drs. Bourne and Jacks exited the fray post haste.

Luckily, classification of Golly and his compatriots in death as a new species was not a problem; no one could argue they weren't human and it was also hard to combat the point when not one specimen but three gigantic men existed. The issue lay in their place in the human evolutionary chain. They were prehistoric men, of dinosaur proportions. This mere fact required a rewrite of the entire line of humans that came afterward. There were now several members of the anthropological community working on a new timeline.

The other mystery was still the head etching that matched the stone carving. Several experts surmised the artwork on the temporal bone had been obviously done at birth, at a time when the skull was at its most malleable. It was a sufficient premise as a first thought, yet, one that could not explain the precision of the drawing with any certitude. Also, a carving done in infancy would have warped with the subject's growth. Every scientist's intellect was being questioned here; if they ascribed to this explanation then Mallory felt they were all dense. She was slightly offended by the theory herself but did not bother to interject an alternative. Suggesting the giant figures were the branded spawns of angels and human women would have cast her into the sphere of professional pariah-hood.

Initially, unbeknownst to her sponsors, it was India who opened that canister of tiny serpents, which grew akin to a three-headed chimera as the days passed. A long time after the debacle of her and Nigel faded, the fellow students came to be so-so friends. India was satisfied with a relationship that affected her so little personally, and therefore, sometimes they met for a coffee or pint at a local pub. On one such outing, she happened to mention to her *friend* a story that her zealously religious, old aunt had told her—a fantastical tale of the fallen angels. Apparently, what these once divine spirits did, which caused them to be cast out of Heaven was to have sex and procreate with human women. India's blather might have devolved into nothing if she had not added that the resulting offspring were said to have been giants.

By this point, practically everything about the project had been made public. Numerous papers were published. There had even been a documentary film crew on-site recently; however, it would be years before there was any commentary added to that footage. Even if every social scientist and forensic biologist pooled their efforts into answering all the questions on this one project alone, uncertainties would exist for a long while. As mentioned, there were various teams and professionals working on the different aspects of the discoveries: the semiology of the carvings, the timeline of the findings as well as the ramifications for an entire currently accepted anthropological human history and of course, the biology of the specimens themselves. It would be difficult to classify any one of the particular challenges as the biggest conundrum—as each influenced the other—but even the lay scientifically-minded person would pause when considering there was soft tissue found on a relic claimed to be several million years old.

There were many casual oglers as well as some not as ignorant gapers. Nigel, for one, visited the site every so often to catch a glimpse—probably now really regretting his rash decision to leave the project. He frequently took snapshots of the site and submitted commentaries to the local paper, which were readily accepted since the project was the biggest news around Gwellen and all its neighboring towns. After India's far-fetched tale, he began to make suppositions of a long-lost past, a time when humans and angels in human form co-existed, effectively opening the gateway to a debate between evolutionary theory and religion. He went on to claim authority on the subject by stating his current doctoral path was focused on this controversial topic.

Mallory, cringing inwardly and out when the first article was followed by a second and then a third, was repeatedly stunned by the idea that Nigel had made the connection on his own. She had doubted his capacity to concoct the elaborate scenarios he put forth in the newspaper. But, even though she didn't like the situation, she had obviously misjudged him. What was more concerning being that the twist he publicized did not bode well for their project going forward; apparently, it was too much to expect to have no other obstacles be set in their path.

When she made an offhand comment about his "absent but pervasive ability to annoy" in Paisley, Grey, and India's presence, Grey conjectured, "He's the sort that likes things handed to him on a platter; not sure who dished this particular interpretation out for him, but he didn't arrive at it on his own. I'm certain of it." He cast Mallory a meaningful glance. "And unless his source is an ecclesiastic, he'll run out of material soon enough. He seems to be getting desperate already. A couple of days ago, I restrained myself from doing the prat serious bodily harm when he approached me for an interview. He would not have done, not me, anyway, if he had other avenues to fluff the story along further."

India bobbed her head in agreement, relaying what she had told Nigel to spur his idea. "It was just a silly little story my crazy aunty ranted on about once or twice. It never occurred to me the dunderhead would believe such a thing. I should have known really; Nigel'll latch on to anything …" The realization of her comment struck her and she proceeded defensively. "Gah! He thought Golly was an ape!" Then she added timidly, "It'll blow over."

Mallory's eyebrows furrowed as she pursed her lips. She turned to Grey, subtly gesturing toward the doorway. Unhesitatingly, he sauntered out of the tent while a usually composed Paisley gaped in horror. "India, I— I'm— I don't know what to say." Paisley paused to collect herself, yet, her usual porcelain complexion heightened several shades of pink until her cheeks and forehead were aflame. "I am surprised that you would be so careless. Nigel of all people? Have you no sense or judgement? You can't possibly understand how difficult it is to get and maintain funding for a project this size. I guarantee, now that it's begun it won't 'blow over' and you've made it all the more challenging for everyone."

"Sorry … I'm so sorry. The project is public, I told him nothing before that, and we were just chatting," the student said defensively, looking to Mallory for some reassurance she would be forgiven.

"India, an apology won't get you off the hook that easy. Sometimes you have to hear, then really listen, and try to comprehend when there is a lesson to be learned." Tipping her head once, Mallory urged Paisley to continue.

In a much calmer tone, Paisley returned to her lecture. "Let me give you some advice. Regardless of what you think of your aunt and her belief system, whether you have faith in something entirely different or none at all, no one cares so long as you keep religion and science separate on a professional level, even in a soft science such as anthropology, which isn't deemed worthy of that label by many. When you blur that line, there's no going back because science cannot explain religion and vice versa, not to any acceptable or comprehensible degree. They can coexist, but only complementarily in an individual's personal life. I hope I'm making myself clear."

The student nodded morosely, commendably sitting there listening, all the while, looking as though she wanted to cry.

"I just want to make sure that you get it that Dr. Bourne isn't reprimanding you for having told us. It shows a depth of character that you did. However, in order to be a truly strong *and mature* person, you have to accept the consequences of your actions as well," Mallory said gently.

India lowered her head further and clasped her hands. "I promise I won't speak to Nigel again."

Both Paisley and Mallory shook their heads. "Oh, India, you *don't* understand. This is not about Nigel, at all," Mallory began to explain. "He is who he is and will do what he thinks is right. We're talking to *you*; this is about *you*. And I hate to say this but if you can't grasp that then we're going to have to dismiss you and it won't be because of what you said and to whom you said it. It will be because you opened your mouth in the first place. And truthfully, I'm tired of repeating myself."

India's head jolted upward and she looked at her sponsors, one after the other, in questioning surprise.

"You just cannot go around blithely making remarks or telling stories that are inciting to the work we do. It's not, I repeat, *not* the same as having a philosophical conversation while doped as you gorge on chips. Chit-chatting about angels and very real giants in the same breath is not something professionals do," Mallory added with a subdued note of exasperation.

"We don't want your remorse. As Dr. Jacks said, I want you to hear, listen, and learn. We've placed trust in you and you've violated that trust. More than once it seems. And, apparently, you have shirked the lesson that came just before your second chance, as well. Once and for all, don't blame Nigel or anyone for poor judgement on your part. Acknowledge it! Address it! I'll just finish by saying, there is no such thing as a 'silly little story' from the Bible. That would mean, there isn't one person out there in this vast world who would believe it, and do you know how many people take the words of the Bible as truth? Millions upon millions. It will not look well on you for dismissing the intellect of a single of those persons. Again, professionally speaking, find your line, India and do not cross it, not even when you're inebriated."

With all her diligence while working, the respectful countenance she showed her peers and superiors, and the ability to follow instruction, the student lacked intuitiveness. Mallory looked at Paisley doubtfully but hoped India finally understood. "We still consider you a valuable member of our team, however, make no mistake, the third strike … will be your last with us. You were smart to come back the first time. This project will get your career off to a blazing start. Remember that."

The doctors rose from their seats, signifying the end of the conversation. India remained seated, smiling meekly, and bobbing her head.

To Each Their Own

†

F OR SEVERAL WEEKS, the crew did their best to avoid the building public interest. The site was beginning to turn into a circus. On an ordinary Thursday evening, Mallory climbed into her MG; the motor sputtered, bluffing. "Damn, damn," she swore, thumping the steering wheel. She was upset because Paisley had expressed to her a serious and new worry that Mallory hadn't considered.

They were the originals, the founders of this astounding case; there wasn't a person in the world who could nix the project now, but there were those who could change it dramatically. And all because Everett received another letter from an influential figure in London. The person claimed they were making a mockery of science when, in fact, none of the doctors was a party to Nigel's rants. Members of the team had not even been interviewed—having successfully avoided any questioning about the project from the media. It was that the Bible had been quoted on numerous occasions, in connection with their project that caused this person to take exception. Somehow, the correlations being made were still their fault.

"A little while ago we were debating whether India should stay on the team; we gave her another chance," Paisley had said chewing her bottom lip. "I'm really concerned, Aly; we may not be granted the same opportunity. Everett says BIAI is being pressured to send in a project assessment team. Since LEMM is still the primary administrators on paper, we can't be dismissed altogether. However, BIAI, as the majority funding sponsor, they can reallocate their stake with anyone they want."

As she drove down Kraken Road, she pondered why it mattered. In the end, people would believe what they wanted, even if they were presented with counter evidence. On a personal level and as a whole, belief was stronger than science, although, for many, their philosophy was derived by a process of scientific elimination. Ironically, people could say offhandedly, "I believe," but when it came to anything labeled under the umbrella of religion, many scientists chose to discount it simply because they had not *seen* the proof.

To each their own, she thought yet again. However, she knew this was easier said than accepted on a professional level. There was still so much to do and while Dr. Brandt held a good deal of sway with BIAI, the writer of the nasty letter was a board member too, and a huge financial backer of the Institute and therefore, LEMM. There was nothing for it—they had no recourse.

Asking Nigel to just stop was pointless on many levels. Throughout the region and progressively further, from Lands End to Portreath, he had gained quite a following, from which he received a decent bit of attention and the notoriety he craved. A mere seven miles from St. Ives and thirty-three miles from the dig site, for all the buzz, Ivers might as well have been Gwellen itself. St. Ives was, unfortunately, Nigel's hometown, and for the first time ever, Mallory wished the college were not so very close to home. She was thankful she did not socialize;

she'd already been approached by Nigel's *fans* often enough. And now this.

That was no solution. He wasn't the sort to desist anyway; not from the kindness of his heart. In fact, after his numerous attempts to get back on the project, he would likely relish in the discomfort he continued to cause. He knew, if his followers did not, God and all His accouterments were an anthropologist's nemesis. Indeed, he would not abandon his readers at *The Endish Daily*, especially not since he'd been offered a permanent position on the paper. When the vultures from London media outlets also began to ply him with enticements to join their ranks, India reported that Nigel was seriously considering a career change to anthropological journalism (a reporter), a very small niche toward which he had already made large strides.

Mallory didn't care where Nigel went or what he did, she just wanted to carry on with her job—her passion—and right now, that wasn't a surety. She was on her way to vent some of this frustration; Grey was her fuse and her explosion. She didn't know when it happened, but it did. She had fallen in love with him and so far beyond reasoning as to be both comforting and disturbing. Despite her stress, a warmth spread from her toes to her fingertips at the thought of him. With all of this in-your-face change, she had altered subliminally as well. Once unable to reciprocate a man's feelings to a certain depth, her emotional attachment to him came naturally, suddenly. No longer could she imagine her life without him.

Stopping at the traffic light a few blocks before reaching his house, she leaned into the steering wheel and glared up at the gloomy skies. Fifteen months ago, she had not cared where she worked; her next project could be in Scotland, Ireland, Wales, or somewhere else in England. She'd even participated in a few projects in Africa and Peru. Now, she abhorred the idea of leaving the twenty-eight square miles of Ivers for a few months at a time, let alone the thirteen-hundred of Cornwall, but she could not accept anything less than her current role on the Gwellen site either. Needless to say, nor did she welcome the idea of being separated from Grey.

A few minutes later, she was tapping the simple brass knocker, and inserting a key into the hole behind a swivel-hinged house number plate. She turned the knob in the center of the door and pushed the heavy door with her shoulder.

"I thought I wasn't going to see you again today?" he asked, pulling her away from the doorway and shutting it. Scooping a large hand around her waist, he lifted her off the ground to kiss her in greeting. This was quite normal for them, as it was easier for Grey to bring her up to his height than it was to bend down constantly to hers, even if she rose to the tips of her toes.

"Is it all right I came by? After the conversation I just had with Paisley, I needed to see you."

"Mm, of course. Come on, let's get you a drink."

Settled on the overstuffed, leather sofa in the sitting room, Mallory folded one leg under her and turned toward him. "BIAI is probably going to send an assessment team to Gwellen and that could mean new management."

"You mean someone other than Everett?"

"I mean a replacement for Everett, possibly, but if it comes to that, then Paisley and I will be the ones most likely to get the boot. That means you and India as well."

"Nigel, that tosser," Grey muttered. "How could India be so dense?"

"I've thought about it enough for both of us and it doesn't even matter anymore."

"No, it doesn't. If Nigel could be silenced with bribes or threats BIAI would have done something about it by now. If they assess our project and conclude the problem needs handling differently, all they will find at the end of the rope is a tighter knot. Standing back from the controversy is the best strategy; choosing an aggressive rebuttal will only fuel the debate. Just you carry on as usual and let those who think they know better deal with it the way they will. Can you do that?"

"I suppose." Hesitating, she gazed at him expectantly and then suggested, "If they demote me I couldn't stay, I'll have to look for other work. But, Grey ... I— I don't want this to separate us."

"Nothing on Earth can. I wouldn't let it." He moved closer, then reached over, and easily lifted her onto his lap. "Mallory, you found Golly. They can't take that away and unfortunately for Paisley and Everett, *they* are project management. Fortunately, you are not that in the same sense, not from the business side. I really think your position is safe."

"Oh! You're right; I'm never part of the *internal affairs*. But Paisley ..."

"At this point, I really do think everyone's wasting their time worrying how to backtrack—as if they could ever make it so Nigel never wrote that first piece. The Gwellen discovery is global knowledge now, and his suppositions have reached a broader audience as well. I can't predict whether Paisley's job is secure, but in the grand scheme of things the whole conflict just needs to play out."

Maybe Conscious

†

MALLORY AWOKE IN the middle of the night, sensing Grey's absence. It wasn't his warmth she missed; she was cocooned amidst the bedcovers but when she turned around, his side of the bed was empty. Pulling back the comforter, she quickly donned a flannel shirt of his that she'd taken to using as a robe. A faint light shone from the down the hall.

Shirtless, he stood gazing out of the sliding glass doors to the back patio and garden. The moon was high and bright in the sky, casting a silver aura around his broad-shouldered frame. Noiselessly she approached. He didn't so much as quiver or bow his head as her arms encircled his torso, nor when she splayed her palms flatly over the muscular ridges of his abdomen. He stood motionless with his arms to his sides for several long seconds, until finally, she felt his hands cover hers. Resting her cheek in the deep divot of his backbone, she listened. His heart beat slow and steady but loudly, overshadowing the sounds of his breath. Heat emanated from the core of his body, pooling at a point under the breastbone. She felt the one palm situated just there dampen while the other remained dry but warm.

"You remember when you asked if my death would mark the beginning of the end and I said that was about right?"

Mallory tucked her nose and chin into the groove of his smooth back, softly kissing within the area of normal-colored pinkish skin. "Yes." She extracted an arm and caressed an inky wing, tracing the blurry outline with an index finger. Perhaps it was the effect of the moonlit backdrop that caused his actual form to appear extra dark and the tattoo seem fainter than usual. He flexed his shoulders as though to shirk her touch and she stepped back. "Is something wrong?" She paused and waited for him to answer but he did not. "Look at me."

He turned, his eyes glimmered as though reflecting a trace of light from somewhere. And they glistened.

"What is it?" she asked again softly.

"I was wrong. My life means nothing to anyone but me and, of course, my family and you. But I'm not the key after all. I awoke just knowing."

"And that makes you sad?"

"In a way." He paused for several seconds before clarifying. "Part of me desperately wanted to believe I could help the Nephilim and their children, myself included … that I would be able to make it so we'd know for certain me and my relatives would not be condemned for a sin we've had no part in … that should not be ours to bear for all eternity."

"But why have you lost hope? What exactly do you mean by you woke up *knowing?*"

"I heard a voice, possibly inside my head, it was only afterward it woke me … a dream without a vision. Although, I cannot say if it was just a semi-conscious thought. My sleep did not feel as deep as it was. The non-voice said, 'Accept that you are human and only that, like any other person.' That was all, but enough."

"I didn't realise *you* were under the illusion you were anything else."

"My belief in what I've been raised to acknowledge as the family legacy is so strong, Mallory. I suppose I did arrogantly believe I could be theirs and my own saviour." Grey grabbed her suddenly, embracing her in his arms, crushing her to his chest. Instantly she realized she couldn't breathe or even struggle against him. He, however, was incognizant of the fact and his vice grip persisted. Her only recourse was to stomp on his foot before he suffocated her in his arms.

Releasing her—"Oh, God! Sorry," he exclaimed as she gasped for air. Looking down through wet pools, a single tear escaped from the brink of each orb and trickled down his cheeks. "I'm sorry," he uttered again, hoarsely. He was so logical, thoughtful most of the time. Also, he was emotional. Among his other traits, it was this dichotomy she most loved.

She shook her head violently, inhaling deeply. Then stood on her tiptoes, reached up, pulled his head down toward her and gently kissed the tears, tasting the saltiness of them on her lips. "Believe, Grey," she commanded breathily. "Believe you are just human. There *is* hope in the voice you heard … don't you see? Humans have souls. You said you thought you had one and now you *do* know."

He stared at her, motionless, the confusion and grief in his eyes replaced by a dawning realization. Slowly he spoke. "I cannot know if that's actually true. Not in life, anyway. But I think I'm fine with that … because … Mallory, I need you to know, I love you. Please tell me you will allow me that."

"I suppose," she said, smiling crookedly. "Now hold me and mind those muscles don't flex while I'm within them," she added, pointing at his sinewy arms. "And you don't have to be special for everyone, but you are, so much so, to me as well."

Graceless Girl

†

EVEN WITH ALL the personal and professional drama going on, the coming weeks were in no way out of the ordinary in that the excavation proceeded; every day a new perplexing question arose as analysis of the findings continued, as well.

The tissue tests, which finally came back from forensics, were a wash amongst members of the scientific community—including from Paisley's and Everett's perspectives it seemed. According to the samples and the laws of decomposition, Golly could be no more than six thousand years old. Yet, the timeline of life on the planet was better understood (and accepted) than what factors, or lack thereof, contributed to the decay of biological matter over that course of time. Furthermore, the contradictions of strata placement and everything scientists knew about prehistoric times told Golly to be millions of years old.

Having read the report and the various correspondences that followed, Mallory proposed, "I don't know, maybe we should pause for a minute and consider what exactly the facts are and what is fiction, or rather, the definitions of fact and fiction. I—"

To which, Paisley intervened quickly, "Aly, let's not go overboard. I know what you're going to say and isn't it enough

159

that our colleagues—"

"*Our* colleagues? We don't work with them personally," Mallory interjected.

Paisley's brow creased in a mixture of exasperation and stress, "AS I was saying, isn't it enough that our colleagues are now working to rewrite the human timeline in order to include a new species? I mean, it would behoove us to be cautious before throwing another wrench in the works, specifically heaved at Earth's entire history as we know it." She looked at Everett for acquiescence and Mallory decided she would let the subject die for now. Her friend was still obviously feeling the pressure not to rock the boat to a tipping point.

However, Paisley continued, "I even think it best if we stop publishing theoretical articles and white papers. We need to stop making speculations like Nigel and just stick to the accepted framework." She paused. "We've hired someone who will provide the journals with facts and that's all we'll be submitting for peer review going forward."

Mallory was struck dumb for an instant. Paisley did not say, "For now." In fact, she was suggesting Mallory, specifically, stop being an anthropologist. "Well, then what you really meant to say is you think *I* should stop writing since it seems you've gone behind my back and already done something about it."

That day, after hearing Dr. Bourne's preposterous last comments, Mallory squared her shoulders and silently vacated the confines of the tent, suddenly finding the company of her actual "colleagues" unbearable. She would have expounded on her ideas were it not that Paisley made their position clear.

Neither LEMM nor BIAI would be publishing *her* reports anymore. Moments earlier she had assumed they would at least listen, if not support her ideas afterward—as they'd done before. However, now she knew they were unwilling to consider even the possibility of the scientific community's understanding as backward (Mallory's own thinking too, as it was, these many years).

When the tests had come back—Specimen composition: human tissue; Age of specimen: 5700 BCE—along with the poignant disclaimer, "Accuracy of results: 0.001%," she and Grey had discussed it at length. To them, it appeared to be another case of choosing what to believe. Was the current artifact dating methodology credible or was it simply concocted evidence once again represented as fact? Perhaps the natural processes of the many elements involved in decomposition were actually a better marker than some gimmickry designed to age specimens by means of the radioactivity of one atom, Carbon-14. Everyone knew carbon dating was faulty.

For Mallory and Grey, it was easier to accept that Golly and his companions of the grave were a mere six thousand years old than it was to allow the giants to be sixty-million years old with *intact* soft tissue. But, God forbid she assumed people wanted to learn the truth more so than follow a predefined course, on dubious basis or not.

Progressively with each passing day, Mallory could feel the enjoyment of her work slip away. Her friend was right. They couldn't very well challenge everything, but now there were too many opinions she was keeping bottled up—for the sake of what? Wasn't scientific understanding and the resulting knowledge the product of the process of elimination? Every stone unturned—again and again, if necessary.

She also suffered by the rift this caused between herself and her practically lifelong and dearest friend. It was Mallory's fascination with anthropology that had brought them together. After these many years, it was still the subject that bonded their friendship. She was at a loss to explain what she and Paisley were to each other, beyond being work mates now. Furthermore, Dr. Bourne, Paiz, her Paisley, counterpart, sounding board, and close associate wanted her to curb her ideas on the professional front. Mallory was forlorn. The gradual change in their relationship reminded her that her parents were dead and the woman she imagined as an extension of her family had forsaken her for politics. And perhaps they were not even the great friends she imagined them to be.

Seeing her inner turmoil, Grey bid her find her joy in the archaeology and leave the anthropology to those restricted minds who could not allow for change, repeating exactly what Paisley requested of her, but in a different way. He explained that it was for this same reason he had stepped back from the semiological study of the markings on the stones and the giants' skulls. Letting others translate the symbols to their liking was easier on everyone. Ironically, if he were, to tell the truth of it, he would only be lending support to Nigel's stories and that too would capsize the boat, leaving everyone to drown in the mire. Furthermore, he consoled that Paisley's sight would return to her soon when the pressure of the situation was lifted.

Not two weeks after their conversation, when Mallory

was called from the pit mid-afternoon to face an elderly gentleman, by the name of Sir Henry Trenton, it occurred to her to wonder how it was that Grey had known the situation would resolve itself "soon." It had been a month, nearly, since a revised uncertainty had begun to gnaw at her conscience about her friendship with Paisley. When combined, their shared history, beliefs and desires, as well as other commonalities, surely, were stronger than this seemingly insurmountable wave, she thought. However, she stubbornly kept silent on these grounds as well.

From the opening of the tent, she could see Paisley was pacing. When she entered, her friend halted, immediately beseeching her to explain to the visitor that they could have done nothing to stop the force of interest, which had developed from Nigel's commentaries in *The Endish Daily*.

"Please do," Sir Trenton, prompted shortly, however, in a lofty drawl.

At first, Mallory stood dumbfounded without the ready words that might extract them from the inevitable outcome of this visit—everyone's joblessness. She crossed her arms over her chest for a minute as she pondered how to begin. Finally thinking better of her defensive posture, she dropped her arms to the side, also taking a more confident stance with her feet placed slightly apart. Rather than hedging the topic like a meek mouse, she stated the case as such:

"Sir Trenton, I have no care who you are and no clue what you expect me to say on the social implications or, ehm … repercussions of our findings." Her voice was terse; she had no intention of being dragged into the backroom mess.

Paisley's eyebrows shot upward and from behind the small man's frame, she shook her head fiercely.

Sir Trenton narrowed his beady eyes and uttered, "Humphf. Graceless girl." Silently, he reached into his breast pocket, extracted and unfolded a leaflet, and held it up to display the prominent but ghost-like rendering of an angel on the front cover. Behind the rough, familiar sketch was another image, one of the henge stones exposed in its pit.

It was obviously home-printed propaganda. She'd seen the poster version and pamphlet several hundred times now. Being asked to defend against it miffed her even more. "Oh!" She swiped aggressively at her dusty pant legs and scraped her boots back and forth on the ground, pantomiming cleaning them off on a welcome mat. "I didn't realise *grace* was a qualification. I do not recall seeing the prerequisite in my employment handbook. Regardless, my handbook isn't printed off an inkjet, that much I know."

Surprisingly a tiny grin played at one corner of Sir Trenton's thin lips.

Suspiciously, Mallory resumed. "I hope you did not imagine I'd acquired some kind of marketing credential on the sly. For if you saw the adverts pinned about, it wasn't I who plastered them there, nor would it have been Dr. Bourne. The culprit was likely our host; the at once estimable but later revealing himself to be the irritating Mr. Fritchey." She paused and thought *none of this is really Sir Trenton's fault*. She backed away from the brink of her anger but only by a touch. "Sir, I can only politely thank you for your visit but you see we already have our full measure of bystanders who do *nothing* to make our work any easier. Who in fact, contribute greatly to the opposite." She gestured toward the tent exit.

Sir Trenton made no move toward the doorway. Putting her hands together in a gesture of prayer, begging Mallory to take a different tone and tact with her address, Paisley mouthed, "Please, oh please, be nice."

As the gentleman watched her intently, undisguised Mallory cocked an eyebrow toward her friend in return, screwing her mouth in annoyance. She *was* being nice-*er*. Yet, she would be fake no longer and that meant she would not hold her tongue either. "Unfortunately, I'm not an expert in the publicity arena. My interests and expertise lie with archaeology and, Sir, I cannot help what *I* have dug up. In conjunction, my academic profession is that of an anthropologist. I would like it understood: outside goings-on are out of my depth and control."

"I'm sure Sir Trenton isn't interested in—" her friend tried again.

"On the contrary, perhaps a straight answer is exactly why I have come. Certainly, I shall get one once Dr. Jacks arrives at her point. She appears to be on the verge." He stood ramrod straight and proper, in his expensively tailored suit, seemingly unsupported by an ornate, mahogany cane with its ivory, mallard's head handle at his side. His palm flexed and lightly clasped the cane again, yet, a trace of a smile remained on his face.

Paisley rolled her eyes, plopped resolutely into her chair, and gazed absently at the screensaver of her laptop.

Her friend could not see the expression Mallory

interpreted as smugness on Sir Trenton's visage. The small, white-haired, bushy eye-browed man's condescension riled her further. However, she also felt sorry for Paisley. She would have to choose her own route—whether it be a more apologetic or biddable one—but Mallory couldn't in good conscience throw her over the boat beforehand. "Here's my little disclaimer." She smiled thinly, her lips stretched over her teeth. "My thoughts are my own and Dr. Bourne here is in no way responsible for me or what comes out of my mouth. I do not speak for her or Dr. Brandt, for that matter; I speak only for myself."

"Yes, yes. We'll see." Sir Trenton nodded expectantly while Paisley proceeded to prop her elbows on the table and bury her head in her hands, expressing her distress at the situation afresh by slumping her shoulders in surrender at Mallory's next words.

"Now … I'll put it plainly, it annoys me to no end that we, as scientists, must rely on deep pockets in order to make our discoveries—while earning a meager living wage doing so—from what I understand excavations are costly ventures, but that is why I stay out of the politics. Personally, I continue not because of pressures from the *outside*. Discovery and knowledge are my rewards. So, if you've come here with a better solution to the marketing problem then all I can say is, have at it. I do not think you will find fault in what we have accomplished thus far on the excavation side. And if you feel righteous enough to dismiss me from my post because I do not waste time negotiating, nay, cajoling a pissant graduate student like Nigel Dupant then I gladly leave you with the reins of the cart and buggy. It goes without saying; I assume … you have the means to manage the whole damn pony show however you please. There, *Sir*, you have my point and with about as much grace as I can muster."

Sir Trenton furrowed his shocking white eyebrows, skimmed Mallory's figure from the tip of her muddy boots to the top of her bedraggled head and laughed; a loud, boisterous, surprising chortle. The air of the tent filled with the sound.

Paisley raised her head and stared at the man's back in astonishment, then looked to Mallory who shrugged her shoulders questioningly, raising her hands, palms faced upward. She, too, was unaware of what she had said that was so funny.

"Too right, you stay away from all forms of politics, Dr. Jacks," the man said, smiling, and showing teeth that were likely dentures—albeit they were well made enough to be indistinguishable as such. "And you …" He spun on his heels like a sprightly lad to face Paisley. "Continue to manage as you were. Expect no other interruptions or bothers. I shall make certain you have none. Now, if Dr. Jacks will do me the honour, I would like to see the spectacles myself and then I leave everything in your capable hands."

Afraid to undo what she had apparently done, but hesitant to leave questions fluttering about, Mallory asked blatantly, "And what of Nigel? If from behind the scenes the stakeholders expect us still to somehow contain public interest or sway religious beliefs toward more scientific opinions, then BIAI and LEMM can expect my resignation." She made sure to look pointedly at Paisley when she mentioned LEMM. "Because at this point, I'd rather sever my attachment to this project if, in fact, anyone is under the impression I shall suddenly care about what people think when in my mind, they are just plain being illogical."

"You have made yourself quite clear, my dear. I may be old, but my wits are intact. I understand now, with the help of your forthright perspective." He reached over with bony fingers and laid them on Mallory's forearm. "These are two separate matters while the one is a consequence of the other. Perhaps it is best if the 'outside,' as you say, remains in the periphery. If we do not stoke the fire, it will die out on its own."

Paisley rose, coming to stand beside Mallory.

Sir Trenton eyed her critically, simply nodding in acknowledgment of her presence. Turning back to Mallory, he said, "Furthermore, I commend you, Dr. Jacks. You have done what no other has had the gall to do—speak to me as one with a self-moral code, which cannot be bought or threatened. A consequence of money and prestige is oft people do not tell me of the reality. They do what I bid without having the courage to tell me I know not what I demand. I say, 'Jump' and they do not so much as prematurely ask, 'How high?' Instead, most jump repeatedly until they either reach the height I desire or plummet to their own demise. In fact, when it turns out to be the latter, regardless how hard a man or woman has tried, I do not deign to help; for as a businessman, to me, this amounts to a disqualification of his professional character. Thus, if you resign, I would accept the others' as well."

Mallory did not know enough about Sir Henry Trenton to

comprehend the breadth of his influence, but from his manner and speech, he was more than just influential. The little man was powerful.

"Again, Dr. Jacks, a tour if you please. And I would like to hear all of your opinions; something tells me you have some very controversial ideas brewing in that unconventional mind of yours."

Grey Skies

"**T**HAT'S MY GIRL," Grey pronounced blandly when Mallory repeated the altercation with Sir Trenton to him. "Did you really not know who he was?" He continued folding shirts and placing them neatly in the suitcase on the bed. Absentmindedly looking around the room, he disappeared for a moment, presumably to gather belongings from the bathroom.

"Was? I still don't know who he *is*." Mallory said offhandedly, raising her voice slightly just so he might hear her reply from the other room. She knew Grey was worried, but there was no point in inciting the situation further. He would know more once he actually faced the source of his concern.

"I'm sure it doesn't matter. You're you. You would have addressed him the same." He bowed his head and pondered the contents of his baggage. "I've no idea how long I'll be away. Mum says Martine is fine, but I have to see for myself what that means. But just so you know, if I get my hands on the bastard who did this to her I may be detained a while longer, even if I don't get arrested for beating him to a pulp." His mouth curled in a disgusted snarl.

"Go be brotherly, but I'd consider it a personal favour if you came back with your pretty face unblemished and also preferably with all the limbs you were born with still attached to your body." She hesitated before saying, "Grey, I have no right to give you advice on the matter, but I mean it in the best way possible … because I care … your sister needs some mental help. While you're there, you might look into getting her to a therapist. Not that I've met Martine either, but I've never known *or heard* of a person who would offer to pick up drugs from a dealer. Likely, the type would be a very dangerous fellow, to begin with. It stands to reason that this particular character is doubly so, as he hadn't been paid for a fix he'd already fronted. I'm just saying, the idea goes well beyond what a normal person would do as a favour for a friend."

Unlike him, Grey issued a series of profane words as he threw the last of the toiletries into the suitcase. "Oh, I know. Believe me, I know." He smashed the contents down, although the bag wasn't nearly full; it would have closed easy enough without the rough handling. "I have a feeling everything is about to change; partly that is what disturbs me. It's not just this business with Martine."

Mallory nodded. The conversation was a disjointed blend of several topics. Both were aware of the fact, but neither could pinpoint the cause of the enveloping strangeness.

Shaking his head as though to clear his mind he said, "Currently, Sir Henry is the number one benefactor of every single museum in the whole of the United Kingdom—an aristocrat who did not stand idly by just basking in the empty glory of the titles of his forefathers. In fact, his father and grandfather were parliamentary figures who maintained the line but did not bring it any further prosperity. Whereas, Sir Henry single-handedly multiplied the Trenton family's wealth a thousand fold."

"How?"

"By scooping up every scientific publication he could get his hands on and making them credible sources, avenues for reporting on all forms of technology and advancement. Most of what you see, in use, and accepted as fact across this nation is because it appeared in one of those publications first. Hospital equipment and procedures, scientific theories and practices, and so forth."

"That explains a lot. He asked me to issue a paper on henge formations as burial sites. Another for my opinions on how we might alter world understanding of anthropological history as it relates to how we currently evaluate the age of a specimen using carbon dating. I told him I thought decomposition rate study was the wave of the future. He said he would make sure my articles were published in the most esteemed industry journals."

"So you told him ..." He visibly tensed. He removed his shaving kit, picked up a t-shirt, and unfolded it, only to fold it and place it gingerly back in the same place at the top of a neat pile. Opening the small, blue, leather case containing his shaver, charger, and lotion he peered inside and inventoried the contents; closing it and again, situating it between the two rows of clothes.

Mallory shoved the suitcase back across the mattress and moved to sit on the edge of the bed in front of him. Straddling his hips, she pulled him forward. "Mm-hm. I mentioned it was ridiculous to stop questioning the viability of our current methods just because it's common practice. Especially as it cannot be proven as conclusive by a long shot. It's as if saying aspirin across the board prevents heart attacks so if a person takes aspirin they can be assured not to have a heart attack. When in fact, at least, fifty percent of the population, women, should not take aspirin regularly at all."

"I didn't know that," he replied and he reached around her to pull the bag forward.

She swayed sideways, attempting to block the nervous confusion that was driving him to fidget—he was done packing. "He asked if my notions collided with the creation of the Earth or the Big Bang Theory. And I told him, the Earth could still be a gazillion billion years old for all it mattered, we were talking about life and so what if it took only ten-thousand or so for the biology to develop." She crawled a hand under his shirt and up his smooth, muscular chest.

His eyes grew dark under their hooded lids. "No mention of creationism then ... in your conversation?"

"Grey, ... your flight is in two hours. I—"

"You didn't say anything about the remarkably similar story of an apocalyptic flood; a barge of grand proportions holding two of every kind of creature; and a man, his wife and two sons aboard this ship? A story that appears in numerous ecclesiastical texts of various faiths," he interrupted. "How about the fact that Golly, Adam, and Tiny were found in a sedimentary layer coinciding with the time of the flood?"

"Cool your heels. No, I did not; I still think faith is personal, quite a separate thing from what can be proven on the scientific level for human mental consumption. Now focus, man, on the task at hand and bid me a proper farewell. I shall miss you and *want* you to give me something that'll sustain me."

Three Words

†

ALY, CAN WE talk?" Paisley reached out to grab Mallory's hand but decided against it.

"We talk every day, practically. I didn't realise we were asking for permission to speak now," she said without looking up, unaware of her business partner's current state of agitation. She was too distracted by the end-of-the-week task of updating the scheduler program with progress notes to notice Paisley looked as though she was about to cry. Ever confident and composed, she never cried.

"Are we oh-kay?" she hedged and her voice hitched.

Startled, Mallory glanced up to face her friend's guilty expression. She then realized Paisley was finally prepared to address the change in their relationship. Mallory had wondered if they were going to leave things so impersonal. It had been weeks since they enjoyed each other's company, longer than that since they'd shared anything about their private lives.

Deciding it was time to be frank, and without taking ten minutes to get to the point, she pushed the laptop aside and shoved the words off her chest. "When it came to the business side of things, Paiz, I've always trusted you. It made sense because I'm no good with all that. But never, ever, for as long as we've known one another have you asked me to stop doing my job, stop using my brain, to just shut up. To tell you the truth, because you did, I began to think maybe we were best friends—for over twenty years—only in *my* head and all I really am to you is a glorified grad student with *notions*. I guess I assumed you trusted me, as well."

"Aly! I didn't mean to question your judgement. I was just feeling a bit overwhelmed and you know you are as dear to me as my family because you *are* family and my best friend, besides."

"My friend would never have sold out on a principle nor would she have backed away from criticism coming from a *general* direction. She would have refocused the audience, *re*-targeted, *re*-strategised the direction. My friend is savvy like that. She would have fought my case even if I said we'd found faerie dust. Paisley, this project has been our life for a good long while and you asked me, nearly demanded I not do what I do. You went as far as to take the choice right out of my hands. You know— you know I question everything and that's what drives me professionally."

"I know," she said softly, looking remorseful. "I also know we can fight every once in a blue moon, can't we, and come through it? Aly, it would make me feel so much better if you would stop being disappointed in me."

"Yes, but Paiz, I'm going to have to beat a dead horse. If someone doesn't like the way I'm doing my job then she can take that job and ... well, stick it up her keister. I just didn't expect that person to be you, the one belittling me. You know? *Everything* we do *is* supposition. In fact, it *begins* with an educated guess!"

"We're on the same page now. I have to admit I've never

managed a project this size and with pressure from all sides, I didn't realise until afterward that I was being tested and I failed, both you and myself. I've learned, truly I have."

"All right. Give me a hug and let's go back to being normal."

They embraced one another fondly, but afterward, there was a moment of uncertain silence. In the lapse, Mallory ponderously looked down at her feet, not knowing if she should resume work on the schedule or ask after Mr. and Mrs. Bourne.

"I read your article in *Anthroscience Journal*," said Paisley. She wanted to express she was sorry it hadn't been published through LEMM. However, she refrained.

"I submitted it directly to Sir Trenton and he sent it to his people," Mallory said hesitantly, glad for the change of subject but still unsure of Paisley's stance when it came to theoretical disclosures. "It wasn't really a conflict of interest because of his affiliation with BIAI."

"It was— controversial but brilliant. Do you really think intact DNA can be extracted?"

"Yes, from Adam's tissue specifically. As I mentioned in the article, I think it's foolish to disregard the biology. It is no less relevant than the anthropology and in fact, the two are intertwined. Golly's back teeth, for instance, are flatter than human molars; his incisors were blunter as well. That could mean he was less omnivorous than any other human species. He was possibly an herbivore altogether. A hard-scientific study will help draw a clearer picture."

"I've gone ahead and asked the lab to test and analyse the traces of bone marrow. But, let's go back to us. Can we have dinner together tonight—just you and me?"

"I'd like that. Grey should be coming home any day now, but I've missed *you*." She stood on her toes and encircled Paisley's broad shoulders once again, this time squeezing her tightly.

Paisley planted an affectionate kiss on her friend's cheek. "It has been three weeks, how long is Grey planning on staying away? He wasn't too thrilled with what's been going on either. I hope he hasn't abandoned the project for good. Has anything happened between you two? Keaton was wondering as well."

Mallory pulled away and squinted suspiciously at her friend.

"Oh no! Don't give me that look. I'm not butting in, I swear. I was just curious and telling you something maybe you didn't know."

"Regardless of Grey, if Keaton is waiting, he needs to stop. That's his call, though. And Grey and I are just fine, fantastic even. I'm completely besotted, obsessed—whatever and forever, I think. I can't imagine feeling this way about anyone again. To be honest, it scares me a little."

Paisley stared at her in shock. She had never before heard such words uttered from her friend's mouth. She was surprised "besotted," "obsessed," and "forever" were part of Mallory's vocabulary let alone strung together in the same sentence. "Have you told him? Have you actually said the *word* out loud?"

"No. He knows. He told me he did … that he feels that way about me."

"Aly, it's terrific you have such an emotional and mental connection," Paisley said slowly, "but I guarantee you, Grey needs to hear you say it."

"I can't just blurt it out, besides he doesn't expect me to. We've talked about it."

"Rubbish! And yes! Yes, you can. When you're eating with your mouth full and he makes you laugh you almost spray out your food; during sex when you're caught in the moment; when he's looking especially lovely to you covered in workday grime or not, you say it."

Mallory nodded pensively, blushing in remembrance of the day he left. "I'm pretty demonstrative otherwise. God, which would be at ten times a day."

"That there is a sex life that would put the randiest teenager to shame! Where do you find the time? Seriously, though, he probably won't get tired of hearing the phrase."

"It's not that often! I just meant there are many opportunities throughout the course of a single day. Aside from the physical, he makes me laugh, feel things, and always looks amazing to me." Just voicing this much made her crave his homecoming. Although they spoke on the phone daily and video chatted, the virtual contact wasn't nearly enough. It had been maybe fine for three or four days, at tops a week. Today was three weeks and a day since he'd left and there was still no set date for his return in sight—although she had said, she expected him "any day now."

The situation with his sister wasn't easily resolved. He meant to stay in Queenstown for as long as it took for Martine to be settled with a good therapist. He was also trying to organize an intervention with family and real friends, not the leeches who took but offered nothing except trouble in return.

Felled No More

†

QUIETLY SHE MURMURED into the phone, "Another month, or so." There wasn't much she could say. It wasn't as though she could demand he come home. They were attached to one another only by invisible strings. Following a brief echo, there was an extended period of silence.

"You there?"

"Mm-hm."

"Mallory, I miss you terribly but I can't abandon my sister—my family. Martine has to reinvent her personality, her inner self, which probably started going awry when she was just an adolescent." He added softly, "I love you."

She felt like a child. The first thought to enter her mind after he said that was: Oh, but you can abandon me easily enough. Instead, she said, "I know. You should be there and fix what you can. I miss you as well and—" She couldn't tell him for the first time over the phone. Another moment of silence told her one of two things: either he knew what she was going to *try* to say or he was waiting, in anticipation for her to find gumption enough to finish her sentence.

Changing the subject, she said, "So, the latest news on the Gwellen project is we're almost done with the exhumations. There are a couple of stones, which still need to be excavated completely. Would you believe the Biolab Corporation is going to try to clone Adam? Turns out his tissue was fairly complete. Tiny's wasn't too bad and Golly's didn't fare well at all."

"Mm, I read about it. I don't really understand why people need to recreate a thing gone extinct for a reason. They've talked about it with dinosaurs, the wooly mammoth, and other species as well. I heard scientists are even hoping to cross a mammoth with the modern elephant. Why isn't it enough to study remains and then accept the world as it exists with the creatures that are alive now? What good would it do to have a hybrid elephammoth?"

"Who knows? I think it makes small people feel big. It wasn't my intention with my write ups to suggest they go that far, but unfortunately, I've been quoted a few times … in a context that changed the meaning of my words." To illustrate, she intoned in a serious, journalistic voice, "As Dr. Mallory Jacks recently stated in her paper: 'It would be a mistake to overlook what we can learn from the biology of these giant humans.' Thus, along with other methods of assessment, current cloning techniques could very well lend to a modern analytic approach, in this regard."

"And if this thing comes to exist, what do they intend to do with the creature except make it miserable for however long? It's so inhumane, life is life," Grey said angrily. "These *big* people don't think about that; they are small."

"Absolutely. They don't, but lucky for us conscientious folks we have a few powerful people on our side who may see our point."

"I assume you're talking about Sir Henry."

"He's turned out to be quite a staunch supporter of mine. I told him I wanted to write a rebuttal, basically a retraction of what I never said. Maybe, while I'm at it I'll inject some humanitarian rationality for the dead into the argument."

"Good, some people will listen. It shouldn't be easy to just create life in a petri dish, watch it grow into a living breathing being, and then torture the life out of it. People need each other to maintain a balance."

"I think I might use your wording exactly. But, we do it all the time, though, don't we? Create life just to kill it, pour a sauce over it, and eat it. The logic is we're not endangering a species by our wants. Still, that farmed salmon or calf was a living creature as well. It had emotions and felt the pain of slaughter just the same."

"The difference being people are not sustenance, gourmet or otherwise, regardless of whether they existed thousands of years ago. And I doubt they are biologically reincarnating the mammoth as an alternate food source in the battle against overpopulation."

"True that. I almost wish Nigel's following would take up this charge." Now that he had gained the notoriety he desired, Mallory had almost forgotten about the annoyance he'd caused. Nigel still came to the dig site, but his visits weren't nearly as frequent. India and he were still friends and when she happened to mention him, Mallory just happened to have something to do in some other place than the current locale.

"How is that going anyway?"

"Eh, I stay far away from him and the controversy of his angle. As the site supervisor and resident expert on giants nowadays, people always want me to pick sides or else reveal some truth that will make it all clear. I prefer to keep reality and spirituality separate. From what I gather, he's enlisted several ecclesiastics to help him root out the answers."

"Oh, right. Dr. Albright and Father Francis are part of his squad now."

"Mm-hm."

As the conversation progressed, Grey reported that Martine was resistant in understanding that her general approach to life was harmful. The most recent situation aside, the past was the past, and yet she refused to accept she was the same and could very well get into another mess again. Next time the outcome could be worse.

He also recounted a brief encounter with the ruffian, the one who had inflicted the current hurt on Martine when he demanded payment for a debt that wasn't hers. What happened the day of the assault was this: Rufus, the drug dealer, presented to Martine what he conceived as fair terms. Since neither the drug user nor her friend could pay in full, *in cash*, he deemed it within his right, as a businessman having already rendered a product into a customer's hands—a very expensive product with no return policy—albeit illegal, to exact payment by other means.

To Grey's frustration, he discovered that Martine had stupidly credited Rufus's point, for even a minute, even though her consideration was as she said, "Based on a misunderstanding."

Sure, she hadn't *wanted* to pay that way but it would have closed the deal, or so she first thought. It was while she hemmed and hawed over her decision just to get it over with that she found out what her consent would have truly meant. Apparently, Rufus had connections in other shady establishments and this debt would take some time to pay off. He had only been suggesting that he "sample the flavour" so he would be sure to recover his substantial losses. Maybe in the long term, he would even make a little extra from Martine. Of course, with this enlightenment, she hesitated no longer and was soon defending herself against a probable rapist.

Learning the scumbag had called Martine a whore while attempting to violate her body, Grey was even now battling the urge to hunt Rufus down and pummel him to near death. However, he knew the best thing to do was let the police take care of it while he focused on his sister's wellbeing. Besides, Grey wasn't at all certain Rufus hadn't already received a payment of this kind from Cecily, Martine's friend the drug addict. When he mentioned this in passing to his younger sister, he received another glimpse into the naiveté of her mind.

Placidly, Martine had said Cecily was too frail to confront Rufus herself. The withdrawal, for one thing, had weakened her and years of a hard life and living were the reasons why Martine agreed to help her friend in the first place.

Grey didn't know a thing about Cecily's supposed "hard life" but he nearly yelled that her "hard living" was her own fault. Also, nowhere in any dictionary did negotiating and or settling debts by sleeping with culprits on a friend's behalf correlate in any way with the meaning of the word friendship. That Martine would even think to repay Cecily's debt was disgusting as well as unfathomable. Try as he might, a thought crossed his mind more than once: my sister is indeed stupid.

"Since she does not seem able to think of herself, I'm trying to get her to see, instead, that she is abetting these kinds of situations for her friends. Maybe something will click. The whole horse to water thing ... Martine can't go on thinking it's her responsibility to supply a brimming trough to creatures that tend to overdrink. The creatures will suffer more and longer when she can't provide than if they were left to die from thirst. I told her, if she really wants to help, she would stop prolonging her friends' self-induced agonies. And they might actually learn to survive better without her interference."

"If Martine is that sensitive to the plight of others', you could play the guilt trip. You're her *brother*. That must hold some sway," Mallory said, referring to Grey's own injuries. He currently sported a purple, swollen eye and split lip, but on the bright side, the mock eyepatch was better than the broken nose the other guy wore. Grey's appearance was the one reason today's call wasn't a visual one.

"It looks worse than it is. Weird thing is my eye colour has changed ... in my left eye. I'm not sure it will change back."

"What do you mean changed?" asked Mallory, confused.

"My left eye is hazel-ish now and a little more yellow at that."

She could almost hear the quirk on his lips. "And what made you confront this guy? Thought you decided to let the professionals handle it."

"He confronted us. Aberdeen and I were in Cecily's neighbourhood with every intention of getting her side of the story and well, to also get a better idea of the kind of person our sister champions. We approached Cecily's building; the front entry door was locked so we walked around and found another entrance at the side of the building in an alley. It was then Rufus, the bad guy, vaulted from behind a trash bin, grabbing Aberdeen by the elbow and hauling her in front of him. He held a knife to her throat and suggested to lay claim to recompense his losses again where he could. He backed away and then like an eejit he turned around. Then, I was able to attack him from behind. There was no way I was letting him take my sister."

"Was Aberdeen hurt?"

"A little, she was thrown against the wall when I attacked Rufus. She's fine, just a bit scraped up. Aberdeen is a lot like Martine, though, in some ways. She only came with me because she was curious to get another side to the story. Otherwise, she's been hesitant to accept anything actually needed to be done about our younger sister. Now she understands, Martine is not safe, not from herself or her friends. Our parents on the other hand, still need some convincing. This is why it's going to take a while. Martine needs all of us to make her see reason. She's complacent about it all, especially as she's out of hospital and nearly recovered. She's not owning up to the reality she was almost raped. In her mind, she clings to *almost* and rather just dismisses the whole thing now."

"And how did she react when she saw you looking all beaten up?"

"At first, I wasn't going to tell her what actually happened and then realised, no, everyone needs to see things for the way they are. Because it was Aberdeen and me who got hurt, Martine let me take her phone. I've forwarded her email account to my own. I don't bother to reply to messages her friends send her; I'm hoping they get the hint. Cecily, while she sounds mildly regretful, is still likely desperate for her fix. She continues to contact my sister, making attempts to 'Find out what happened' and at the same time, get a reply to her real question. 'Any chance you are able to help me out?'"

Safe and Unsound

†

MALLORY WANTED MARRIAGE. She knew that now. According to her scale of attachment, this long separation from Grey was torture. When he'd left, she thought for the briefest of moments, maybe just maybe, she would revert to her old self. A part of her hoped the attachment she felt to him would diminish a small degree and she would experience a semblance of clarity by the distance. For at the time, before he'd gone, it bothered her somewhat that she felt so strongly for him. It hurt so very bad, still, the death of a loved one; what if something happened to Grey? Could she go on living?

She had imagined herself immune to this kind of love, as well as the depth of it and realized it had been her defense all along; a barrier she erected long ago, perhaps as an only child. Up until the moment she'd met her best friend, Mallory had been the solitary type. Even afterward, in all the years between the age of 14 and 37, apart from Paisley, no one had passed beyond Mallory's invisible fence. Paisley was the same way; however, her wall was erected from self-consciousness. She never spoke of it but, before Everett, Paisley thought herself ungainly and undesirable, despite her good looks. She'd rarely dated, focusing every shred of effort instead on her professional ambitions.

Mallory recalled a brief conversation they'd had as children or rather a comment she'd made that later enlightened her of her friend's insecurities. She had before relayed stories about life in Arizona, her school, and classmates, but one day she mentioned that some of the kids called her "Manly" because she was reclusive, dressed like a boy, and acted like one too, in their eyes. Aside from her father, her most serious role model was a man, Indiana Jones, after all.

Paisley seemed immediately to draw back within herself, saying only, "At least you can change your clothes."

Not understanding her remark at the time, Mallory replied simply, "Why in blazes would I want to do that, kid?" That Christmas Paisley's gift to her was a brown leather hat just like Indiana Jones's. She had also wanted to give her friend a whip but her mom had nixed that idea.

Now that Paisley and Everett were together, irrationally, in a small way Mallory felt like that lonesome child again, except she was no longer content being alone most of the time. Just as she couldn't bring her parents back to life, psychologically, she felt herself weakened whenever she thought of life without Grey. And what she'd said to Paisley was absolutely true. She knew in her soul she would never feel this way again and at the same time, outside of just words, she also wanted hers and Grey's bond to be made as solid as could be, contractual. He would not have left her for two months if they were married.

The need to be with him scared her, but she knew it wasn't abnormal. She knew this was just love. Amidst her personal wants, she absorbed some of his pain as her own, longing to take away his hurt as best as she could. If she could absolve him of it and carry the burden herself, she would. This too was love.

His face had looked so drawn when she'd seen him last. Albeit a high-resolution screen, the camera was supposed to add ten pounds, whereas Grey looked thinner. In a hushed voice, he told her how his father interpreted the dream in much the same way as Grey had initially done. In other words, Mr. McKnight did not share Mallory's opinion that forgiveness was a foregone conclusion of being human. His father went on to say he thought the mental presence's words "Accept that you are human and only that, like any other person" were not to be perceived as a reprieve but instead as a warning. Therefore, once again, Grey was strained with the thought that there was no salvation for his family line, no matter how non-sinful they were and tried to remain until death. Worse still was the idea that there wasn't anything Grey could do, no action he could take; he and his death were not the keys, as they had once thought, and they were all condemned—it was hopeless.

He made a lengthy speech as though lending voice to a storehouse of thoughts; and those thoughts were heart wrenching. Beginning somewhat backward, he explained his current mindset had developed because of Martine's situation. He said he'd never considered a premeditated act before but also had not fully connected that his life was molded by the mere importance of being good. In other words, he hadn't realized how cautious he'd been his whole life. At the same time, he'd always been conscious of needing to be. Having premised his next statement, he then spoke of wanting to kill

Rufus for what he'd done to Martine, wanting the revenge and justice that the police were not able or willing to exact from the criminal. The officials were still trying to capture him on drug trafficking, but on any other channel, they too clung to *almost*. Martine had not, in fact, been raped.

It wasn't the act of committing murder he was afraid of, nor was the cause of his fears the guilt he might feel afterward either. What scared him most was that when a murderer asked God for forgiveness, he would be judged and forgiven if his plea was truthful. Yet, Grey didn't know if he was forgiven even before having done such an awful deed. As far as he could tell, he had committed no sin, lesser or as horrific, his entire life. But, regardless of what he did or his forefathers had done to disqualify him from salvation or what he did or his forefathers had done to earn their place among the damned, he was going to Hell in all likelihood.

Mallory knew the torment he was experiencing was due in a large part to his father's bitter criticisms. She attempted to console him by saying adamantly that she believed every *person* must prove their worthiness in his or her life. He had half-heartedly nodded and then morosely looked away. She wished he wasn't influenced by his father's words, wanted to advise him to disregard the skepticism and negativity, but how could one voice that about a parent? She also wondered if Mr. McKnight was aware of the trauma to which he was subjecting his son. Protectively, she hated the pater familias for being either cognizant or ignorant.

Also, secretly she had hoped all this had been behind them. She wasn't interested in understanding the plight of the

Nephilim or the fallen angels, and definitely did not want it invading her life or philosophy. Having no problem detaching Golly from his past spirituality, it had been easy to push aside the otherworldly ministrations when they jutted their dully-haloed heads. Whether it was Nigel or Grey, who told the story made no difference. She only cared how it bothered him—how it tortured the human him.

"Can't you just live and be happy while you can? I can't see the point in self-inflicting this kind of psychological damage," she questioned, exasperated but moderating her voice to sound calm. "I hate that you're feeling this pressure when there isn't anything you can do about it," she said, a twinge desperately.

He stared at her through the screen, his one green eye, and one gold eye dimmed further. "You nailed it. I have no choice, do I? I guess I will have to try, but I seriously wish I were a bad person so I'd have no doubt left as to where I'm going when I die. I just want to be like, literally to Hell with everyone who is reckless with his or her soul or takes spirituality for granted. Mallory, why are we so blind?"

It wasn't the most enjoyable conversation they'd had these past two months. In fact, just when the situation with Martine was getting better, these new troubles were dampening things again. At least, Grey was finally returning to Ivers next Tuesday.

With this news, the discussion turned to what waited in store for both of them upon his return. The Gwellen project was nearly over. She began to read him her latest paper and he listlessly nodded in intervals. "Grey, everything will be fine when you come home. It will get better, I promise," she said, pushing her tablet aside—he wasn't listening anyway.

"You're promising me my sanity will return? I have no doubt, actually, and should have come home sooner. You are my safe harbour; you know that? I knew the first moment that I laid eyes on you; you would save me from everything bad and myself. I can't wait to come home to you."

"Then why don't you hop on a plane tonight?" she said invitingly.

His extra disheveled, over-long hair, even for Grey, illustrated he was troubled. "I only wish. It feels like a year has passed. I feel off kilter without you— can't you tell?" He ran his fingers roughly through his hair and brought his hand to his lips before speaking again.

Mallory waited patiently for him to give her a reason she must miss him for another week.

"Martine has her first private appointment with her psychotherapist on Friday. Then my parents are throwing a gathering on Saturday to reintroduce her to respectable society. Aberdeen seems to have everything under control, but I'll be staying just a little while longer after the shindig just to make sure things move forward without a hitch. I promise, though, no more delays. My flight is booked and honestly, my bags are already half-packed."

"You took a half-full bag with you when you left. I'm not sure a fourth-full bag is comforting enough for me. Go pack. I know you're going to surprise me and come home early. Might as well be ready."

Interrupted

†

THE WEEK DRAGGED on even more so than normally. By mid-week, the project was just wrapping up and a majority of the dig crew had already departed. India, too, had submitted her project notebook and checked out, returning to her school program with a plethora of content for her thesis. Ironically, even with the altercations they'd had with Nigel, his having jeopardized her participation in the project a number of times, as well as her repeated denial that any relationship other than a strange friendship between them existed, India decided to concentrate her dissertation on the scientific possibility of fallen angels.

While a diligent worker, India's flaky decisions in contrast with her seeming humility after each confrontation left Mallory momentarily puzzled. The student had thought the fallen angel story ridiculous. Mallory brushed it off. She had stopped wasting her time wondering about anyone else's rationale, ready to be done with the archaeological side of the project completely herself.

Now that a nearly identical cast of each of the giant skeletons was on display, in three separate museums—with Golly, Goliath's copy, encased in a glass crypt in LEMM's atrium—the end was in sight. The real artifacts were safely stored in controlled environments (to prevent further deterioration that exposure to air would definitely incite) closest to where primary studies were being done. The actual Goliath was therefore in London, Adam in Edinburgh, and Tiny in New York City.

Monday morning of the following week, Mallory, Paisley, and Everett walked the site, working backward from quadrants thirteen through one, slowly assessing what cleanup needed to take place before the excavation project was officially closed. The tents and structures, equipment and tools would be removed and the few remaining helpers would return to their homes and families in whatever part of the country they lived.

A new crew would enter the scene to regrade the land, which was twenty feet below what it had been at the starting point of this project two years ago. Once the leveling was complete, a horticultural group would come in and re-sod the lawn.

As a national treasure now, the stones would be turned into a commercial venue—stairs installed, tour companies would be allowed. Mr. Fritchey would be either bought out of this portion of the property or recompensed in some minuscule way for the expensively driven traffic to his land. The former was most likely to be the case; however, Mallory was certain Mr. Fritchey was under the assumption the latter would be the way of it.

The farmer was probably anticipating a life of leisure from this point forward. He would no longer bear the expense of advertising; he would only reap the cash from sales of tickets and possibly merchandise. Plush toys of angels and henge, photographic books, screensavers on those cool holographic qcode encrypted business cards, probably danced in his head. Perhaps he envisioned passing his days drinking his morning coffee as he nibbled at a well-crannied muffin, or eating a sandwich during lunchtime at his picnic table while greeting a constant stream of guests. He'd boast about his discovery with visitors from all over the world, and they, in turn, would reward him with stares of awe and ready compliments. Daniel Fritchey was in for a wake-up call.

Before it came to that, the doctors would finalize their plans so as to be well out of the picture and drama sure to ensue. Furthermore, Mallory decided to take a furlough from archaeology for a while. After her arguments on why Adam should not be cloned were published, a lively debate had begun on the role of scientists as providers of knowledge and instigators of advancement versus that of responsible humanity. Thus, Dr. Jacks meant to gather all she knew and had published about anthropology and the Gwellen project, in particular, into a book. Even now, the fire of action was doused, but the embers still glowed brightly for some. The genetics projects were halted and if Mallory had anything to do with it, any future request to clone a subject of an extinct species would always be denied.

The Gwellen project catapulted Mallory's career and credibility. Although she was by no means arrogant, she was aware that it was within her power to extinguish the sparks altogether. She could not forgo the opportunity; she had to push her point home.

Grey would return tomorrow, his flight to arrive just after one o'clock in the afternoon. She meant to be at the airport to meet him and share the exciting news: as he resumed his studies, she too would be delving into academia. Finally, she would tell him she loved him and then propose they be married on Saturday, September 15, 2019. She slipped her finger into the ring in her pocket, the engagement band she intended to present to him tomorrow night at dinner, at Mantra; the location of their first date. It had been safely ensconced amidst velvet backing, inside the black leather box with fine gold borders on its lid, but Mallory removed it for courage.

While a woman proposing to a man wasn't unheard of nowadays, she knew it could be no other way with them. From the beginning, she had been adamant that Grey not push nor should have he any expectations of a happily ever after between them. Therefore, their relationship would evolve only if she made a move forward in that direction herself.

Planning wasn't her strong suit, so she enlisted Paisley's help with an agenda of things to do. Apart from the obvious, get the ring, she'd also spoken to the owners of Mantra and made all of the necessary arrangements. Although Rupa would be present as hostess and her brother, Ajay as their waiter, the whole restaurant was to be reserved for only two diners, Mallory and Grey.

The current dilemma she nervously pondered—as she fingered the ring and walked in the haze of distraction beside her companions—was when to tell Grey she loved him. Wise Paisley advised she say the phrase aloud a few times, just to make sure it *could* come out *and would* when she wanted it to. The first time, Mallory stuttered, "Luh-ove." It wasn't that she could say the word, it was just that she'd never said it before in any truly, meaningful way. "Good morning, Love," "Would you be a love" or "I'd love—" were common enough phrases in her house growing up, but she couldn't recall having used the exact phrase "I love you." Thus, now every time she thought, *I love you*, she felt heartache as she automatically translated it to past tense.

Also, should she say it to him at the airport when they greeted one another after nearly a three-month separation, or sometime after that but before arriving at the restaurant? She didn't want to blurt it out over dinner, did she? Maybe he'd make her laugh like Paisley said and she'd just spit it out. Regardless, it needed to be voiced before the proposal, that was for certain.

"Mallory!" an alarmed Paisley practically yelled, shocking her best friend out of her distracted stupor.

"Wuh— What? I'm listening. Ehm ... I mean what'd I miss?" Mallory grinned crookedly. At the stricken looks upon her friend's and then Everett's faces she tried apologetically, "Has the loo been dismantled already?" Paisley slid an arm around her friend's narrow shoulders.

"No, Aly, my dear; it's Grey," Everett said gravely with an undertone of urgency, raising his hand, and pointing toward a scene a short distance away.

Mallory followed the line cast by his finger. "What about—" A quick lump formed in her throat and the only sound she emitted thereafter was a single, nonsensical croaking *meew*, like a squeaky hinge. She was conscious of what she was seeing, but somehow, it didn't seem real. Her hand stilled in her pocket and she became acutely aware of the ring lodged securely around the base of a now sweaty thumb. Her body, too, had frozen mid-stride. In confusion, Mallory squinted sideways up at Paisley. Whereas, her mind and heart raced toward Grey, screaming in fear.

Once more gazing ahead, the stillness of his body lying on the ground and the black stain that spread out around it made her stomach lurch suddenly. She shook herself out of Paisley's embrace and finally, she ran. As she bent beside him, failing to notice any of the shocking details of the scene, least of all that the shape of the blood-soaked stain seeping into the earth, framing Grey's mangled and damaged body, was so very much like the one upon his back.

Black Thoughts

†

WHEN PAISLEY SPOKE to her, Mallory heard only one or two words of each sentence her friend voiced. She stared blankly at the front door, expecting, unrealistically, for Grey to walk through it while trying to decipher meaning from Paisley's words. She could not get her brain to work. "Eat." "Sleep." Instead, the few words that repeated incessantly in her head with devastating meaning were clear: I never said, "I love you."

As though toward a ghost, Mallory turned to Keaton, who was sitting quietly on a kitchen stool watching her. "Indy," he hedged. "Mallory?" he asked again with barely masked worry written on his face. He waited for her to show some sign of response and then turned to his sister, raising his eyebrows questioningly. Paisley mouthed, "I don't think she's slept." To which, Keaton morosely nodded.

They buried Grey in Lone Fir Cemetery three days ago. Since then, Mallory had spent more hours standing in front of his grave—one so fresh the soft dirt mound bore the distinct pock marks of rain droplets as though pelted by bullets from a BB gun—than she had in her own home. At the funeral, she'd finally met Mrs. McKnight, the proxy mourner for Grey's entire family. Mallory was angry they didn't all come and glad since she couldn't have faced his father anyway, yet this too was not a fact she could truly enjoy. Although the man did not kill her would-be future husband she might have assaulted him all the same for making Grey miserable the past few weeks—the last several hundred hours of his life—and for harassing a good and godly soul, ironically, his entire adult existence.

Mrs. McKnight was a pretty woman; a gentle lady who took Mallory's small hand in her even smaller one and brought it to her tear streaked cheek. She said softly, "While my husband, Abernathy, has his beliefs, I have my own. I believe Grey is safely in Heaven watching over us, especially you, Mallory. Through you, I shall say goodbye to my lovely boy. When he comes to you, tell him I said so and that I shall no longer pray for him. I am that sure he doesn't need it. Ask that he pray for his father; Bert does not know what he does."

At the time, the meaning of what his mother said was too much to think about. Yet, when Mallory visited his grave, she could think of little else. It was for this reason, she stayed there for such long hours. The past disappeared and what remained was hope that she would see him again if only to relay Mrs. McKnight's message. Illogically she imagined he would appear somewhere in the vicinity of his body.

Paisley's garbled voice broke the silence again. Mallory shook her head, stood abruptly, and meandered away, leaving her friend standing there in the middle of the living room. What was the point of being polite? she thought as she came to a stop in the center of the hallway. She couldn't care about that, for she felt only a hollowness.

Grey had not appeared. Part of her wanted to be upset that another McKnight had lied while a piece of her mind grasped at the rationality that wouldn't come. Looking toward her bedroom she realized she hadn't slept. Suddenly, Paisley's words made sense. Rather than walking toward the room to do just that, she turned back around and again glanced placidly at her friend. She couldn't even remember where the past three days had gone.

"Paiz, I can't ... I— ehm, to tell you the truth, I'm not sure ... I heard what you said. I was off somewhere," she choked out.

"Mallory, sweetheart," Paisley pleaded; worried her inconsolable friend was doing a fair job of quickly wasting away from grief. She scanned Mallory's face with a softened gaze. There was a sheen to her friend's cheeks, forehead, and chin, evidence she was unrested, but, otherwise, there was no mark to show that she had released even a tear of her obviously, deep sorrow. In fact, the usually forthright woman looked grimly disconnected from reality.

"Hm?" Mallory uttered, despite having zoned out again. Before he'd left for New Zealand, even though they couldn't know what the future held in store, they'd both sensed a change was coming. Then early on during his absence, that odd feeling of uncertainty had perhaps driven her desperate need for commitment; the same need she had also hoped against. She was aware the growing depth of her attachment to Grey had been weakening her previous emotional independence and still, she'd allowed it to creep its way into her heart. Over the past two months, a dependence had firmly lodged itself in her core anyway.

Grey was tortured by his personal demons and now, her

mind worked to comprehend how she could carry on with her life—burdened with her own torments. Her mother and father and her only love … all of them were gone forever. She was alone. *God, was it true? Oh God, it was true.* Her head began to buzz; questioning where he was now. Did she truly believe, like his mother, that he was in Heaven? Or was he condemned as his father insecurely thought? Collapsing into the armchair, again, she shook her head adamantly, as though she were having a conversation with the detestable man himself. Was that why he didn't come to her as Mrs. McKnight said he would?

"I was saying, come with me."

"What? Where?"

"Come home with me," Paisley repeated. "Let me take care of you, if only for a little while. A few days, Aly."

"Yes. I mean, no."

"You're coming with me if I have to carry you."

Keaton rose and slowly approached Mallory.

"Why?" she asked looking up at the looming frame, who was holding out his hand.

"Because I mean to feed you, make you take a bath, and tuck you into bed. And call me selfish, I want to be there when you cry."

Cry. She couldn't, no matter how much she wished she could. Her grief was stuck in her throat. It hurt her chest and compounded by earlier sorrows it would never go away. Instead of explaining, she was certain there was no release for her, she said, "Paiz, I'm not hungry." As an afterthought, she added, "I ate." Surely, she'd eaten.

"Oh, you did? What was that then?" her best friend asked

skeptically but still gently.

Mallory paused a long while to think. "Just leave me alone," she murmured.

"I will not."

"Indy, you know we can't allow you to just crawl into whatever morbid little hole you can think up. It'll do you no good."

When Mallory failed to respond, it was Paisley's turn to leave the room. Within minutes, she returned with a small bag presumably packed with a few necessities. "Keaton will come back if needed later," she announced. She placed Mallory's phone into her own purse and tossed the house keys to her brother, then they both made to escort their friend toward the door but Mallory stood robotically, going along without any further prompting.

The Giant Race

†

SHE STAYED WITH Paisley for two weeks before broaching the subject of moving back to her own house. Besides entirely too much coddling, she didn't particularly enjoy the bouts of tentative psychoanalysis, overly gentle attempts to distract her—as though she were fragile—, or the air of forced cheerfulness at times. However, she made the mistake of trying to convince her friend that she needed to get away from Ivers, altogether.

Of course, Paisley wouldn't have it and reneged support of her houseguest returning to her own home. As stand-in mother, she knew firsthand that if her charge were to find an escape from her reality it was very likely she would slip into depression. The mourner didn't seem to need an excuse; her grieving was still on the brink of disaster.

Therefore, Mallory stayed another week before packing her now many bags, calling India of all people to drive her— her only other option being Keaton—and returning to the Jacks residence without asking for permission. She'd planned her rebellion to occur while Paisley was out with Everett, which wasn't too difficult since the two were often together nowadays.

As a result of her unapproved departure from the birdcage, the still-turned maternal Paisley dropped by

209

unannounced and often. She also called Mallory incessantly when she wasn't "keeping her company" or in Mallory's kitchen making lunch or dinner.

While it was true, she was still in no fit state to care for herself—sleeping sporadically for a few short hours over a period of days, forgetting to nourish herself on a regular basis and skipping all manner of hygiene and housekeeping from time to time—Mallory found her friend's hovering stifling. The problem was she didn't want to live; she knew it and so did Paisley.

One day, she changed the locks. When Paisley tried the key, rattled the doorknob, slammed repeatedly at the knocker, and finally walked around the outside of the house, peeking through all the windows, Mallory stood with her hands on her hips in front of her living room window and yelled, "You're driving me mad I tell you!"

"Christ!" Paisley shouted back. "Don't you ever bloody scare me like that ever again! Now, stop being a prat and let me in."

"Only if you promise to take a chill pill," she said, leaning down to prop herself against the windowsill. Drawing the features of her face toward the center of it as though she were angry, she glared at her over-protective friend.

Paisley pointed off in the distance, vaguely and enthusiastically gesturing toward the door.

"Ehm, first, I'll have your oath, then there will be some ground rules, and *then* I shall open that door." She held up a single finger. "One." At the gesture, her self-imposed guardian bellowed; doubling over, gripping her abdomen, she kept on laughing.

"Paisley Bourne, you behave yourself or I shall divorce you just like kids in the U.S. might do their parents."

Paisley slowly composed herself but a very self-satisfied grin continued to play on her lips. These sparks of Mallory's attitude were rare nowadays.

"As I was saying … you will call before you come over, at least until you normalise again. Two," she pronounced. "You'll stop mothering me."

"No."

"What do you mean, 'No'? The rules are non-negotiable, Dr. Bourne."

"Good. Because I'm not negotiating. You and I both know I have to do what I have to do until you gain your sanity back. Open the door, Aly, and we'll have a conversation like adults, that is *after* you prove to me you can start acting like one."

She backed away from the window and dropped down on the sofa, crossing her arms petulantly over her chest. She squinted and pursed her lips menacingly again, challenging the superheroine on the other side of the glass.

Paisley disappeared from the view. Mallory waited, not knowing if her friend was playing some trick. Within a minute, Paisley returned and plastered a poster against the window glass. At which, of course, Mallory rose to take a closer look. An image of a man standing next to a parked car dominated the scene. His digitally stretched and contorted figure dwarfed the vehicle. The heading read, "The Giant Race," and the byline underneath stated, "Genetic research could bring him back to life. Are we ready?" In subscript, the amateur flyer also asked,

"Will Dr. Mallory Jacks fire the starting pistol or will she maim the contestants?" Silently, she went to the front entrance and pulled open the door.

"Care to join the opposing fray once again?" Paisley asked, grinning sheepishly, perhaps feeling guilty for using political tactics to provoke her friend to rejoin life.

In truth, Mallory was unmoved by the crappy poster. As though all it took was one measly, poorly framed nudge to make her go "Ah! I have a purpose … life is suddenly worth living" or angrily provoked into it. What she really wanted was to let the idiots of the world dig their own graves, taking the clueless and unreactive along with them. However, she was cognizant enough to know that if she became *involved* with something, with life, Paisley would at least back off. Thus, she would work, eat, and sleep, since this is what seemed to be required of her. In doing so, the acting mother would be appeased, perhaps demoting herself to the ranks of sister instead.

Paisley set about making lunch, which to Mallory was breakfast while the latter shuffled through notes shoved into desk drawers. She then collected several books and journals off the bookshelves in her father's former study, plopped them down on the kitchen counter, and began pantomiming diligent effort. When the cook wasn't looking, she doodled Grey's name into the margin of an under sheet of her notepad. Pausing, with pen poised and the sheet of paper blocking Paisley's view she faked that she was thinking. She opened a magazine or book and browsed blindly as though looking for a particular article. Periodically, bending her head to her notes to jot down an idea, she instead drew a heart shape and slashed it through with a thunderbolt of black, severing the romantic symbol in two.

Luckily, her notepad had some useful points that had already been compiled during a previous strategy session. Over a simple meal of scrambled eggs, buttered toast, and coffee, she read aloud the tact she'd devised against the cloning of Adam, also announcing the advantages of genetic replication as addressing both sides often made for a well-rounded argument.

Satisfied with the ruse, Paisley rose to clear the dishes and clean up. She next hovered around the house, tossing clothes from the hamper, linens from the bed, and towels from the bathroom into the laundry machine.

Ignoring her friend's ministrations, Mallory continued to sketch. For the first time in weeks, as she subconsciously flanked each side of the heart with a wing, her vision cleared enough to picture the vivid appendages that had seemed to bleed out from Grey's prone body. She gasped and her heart felt for a moment as though it stopped beating. As soon as Paisley left, she would go to the cemetery. At the very thought, the loud drone from the vacuum cleaner assaulted her ears. She stomped up the stairs and flailed her arms in front of the bedroom doorway to get Paisley's attention. The noise stopped.

"I need to concentrate; I'll be in my— in the study." Now, even four years since her parents' death, with the grief of Grey's death compounding and renewing that pain, she couldn't even manage to utter three words "my dad's study" without feeling the choking tightness climb up her throat. She abruptly turned her back to Paisley and stood still, bracing herself against the doorframe, inhaling deeply a few times. Her upper body visibly shuddered with the effort.

She squeezed her eyes shut and gritted her teeth, bracing herself as if the noise had returned. Just as suddenly she began to walk toward the landing. "And, Paiz I barely use the upstairs, you know that, nor am I regularly dragging in filth downstairs either. You don't have to clean every time you come by … your hovering *and* hoovering is truly annoying," she said too calmly, still with her back turned.

"Unused rooms get dusty … I was only tidying," Paisley said guiltily, thinking it was the room she was cleaning (which was partly true), a reminder, that caused Mallory to relapse into grief. Quietly she shut the door of Mr. And Mrs. Jacks's former bedroom behind her. Carrying the vacuum, she followed Mallory to the lower level. Once she'd stashed away the appliance in the hall closet, she found her brave friend once again in the kitchen, meticulously but absently gathering up the materials from the countertop. Maybe Mallory did need some alone time so she could stop acting brave. "I might as well leave now, but you'll give me a set of keys?"

"No. The den window doesn't lock. In the case of emergency … break glass," she said in a clipped tone, her patience restrained. The window was very small; she didn't expect Paisley to use the access in any other situation.

"All right," Paisley said uncertainly. "I'll come back at six."

"I'm fine. Get on with your life. Not only can I make myself food, I can take care of myself. Although I thank you for it, please go back to being my friend … not my mother,"

Mallory said. All the fight had faded from her voice.

"Aly, are you sure? How can I be certain you—"

"No one can be sure of anything, Paiz. I know that more than ever now."

Unmarked Grey

✝

T HE RAIN HAD stopped. Still, the saturated surroundings pelted her with droplets as the wind whipped through the cemetery and its aisles of graves. Mingled with the fine mist on her cheeks were now streaming tears. It had taken that surreal but all too vivid image of the wings around Grey's dead body to finally inspire this emotional release.

There was still no marker atop his grave. In a week's time, he would have a tombstone and it was to be plain. While she was here, Mrs. McKnight had chosen it from the funeral home's catalog. She explained that although they were a Christian family to mark a probable Nephilim with a cross was too arrogant.

Again, Mallory pinned the blame of another insult on the father since, at least, the mother had said she believed her son in Heaven. *Then again, what mother wouldn't say that.* Had Grey and Mallory been married, even though she wasn't devout, she would have exalted him to Heaven with a giant crucifix for the opposite reason; to pronounce his salvation to the world and proclaim him as the savior of fallen angels to his Heavenly jury.

As she stood there placidly swallowing her anger, suddenly she thought she felt his presence. Through the gloom, his scent seemed to waft around her, enveloping her. She grabbed at herself, clutching her upper arms tightly, hugging the mist to her. Yet, she saw nothing. Softly she spoke, telling him first Mrs. McKnight's message, specifically leaving out the prayer request for Mr. McKnight. Obviously, she was still bitter and felt the man needed to pray for himself. *Abernathy*. She disliked the name and at the same time felt sorry for all the other Abernathys of this world.

Now the tears would not stop; they cascaded down her face. She could taste the slight saltiness and relished the flavor. Collapsing from inside out, she knew her mental state of mind was far from healthy, far from just grief-stricken. And so she told him. Although solemnly, she asked, no, demanded Grey return to her—not just come to her every now and again in this uncertain way but return fully in body and spirit. If he did not, she told him, she was readying herself to come to him, where ever that may be.

A mild electric tingle tickled her fingertips and she tightened her hold on herself, pressing the pads of her fingers into her arms painfully as though trying to push the vibration further into her body. She'd only felt that prickle when touching Grey. Only, the feeling went entirely away in an instant. Mallory wanted to scream but the energy to do so escaped her. Instead, her knees buckled and she crouched weeping, her pants becoming as cold, wet, and dirty as they had during the early days of working at the Gwellen dig site.

Slowly she rose, calmly wiped her cheeks and under her nose with the sleeve of her jacket, and strolled out of the cemetery, feeling unhinged.

Unreasonable Voices

†

HAVING APPARENTLY DRIVEN herself to the cliffs a mile away from her house, from the front of her car she stared out at the usually cerulean blue ocean, muted in color today by the dull grayness of the sky and the fog wafting toward the bluff. She couldn't recall having the notion of coming here nor could she fully comprehend her motive. It was as though her subconscious was, in fact, readying her to join Grey. At the same time, it diminished the vague window of time she had given him to respond to her demand.

The strange part was that she must have been somewhat aware. This was one of the few, fairly level access roads to the ocean, but her MG would have propelled forward off the cliff had she not turned off the ignition well in advance of where the vehicle was parked now. She shouldered the door, got out, and walked absentmindedly toward the edge of the crag, an outcropping of wildflowers brushing her legs the closer she came.

You have not seen the last of your beloved.

Mallory halted mid-stride, spinning around slowly. The wind muffled her ears but she wondered: Who was it who spoke? She couldn't have possibly said that to herself and it wasn't Grey. Neither of them would have phrased the promise that lay in those words, in exactly that way.

"Really?" she shouted. "Bugger all!" she yelled next, figuring she had nothing to lose. The voice could have been a figment of her crazed imagination. "I'm bloody going insane here, and that's all you can ruddy well give me?" she asked the sky. She waited but no response came.

Stomping toward the cliff like a petulant child denied a lollipop she exclaimed again. "Well, effin' just great! Why don't I just careen myself off the bloody face of this godforsaken planet right now anyway?" She gestured abruptly, pointing toward the land's end. "The effin' world is going to Hell in a hand-basket soon anyway. No?" Surprisingly the tantrum felt good. Ten feet from the precipice, she sat down and allowed herself to laugh hysterically until her sides hurt. Indeed, she was going crazy.

Then crawling forward on a grassy opening a smidgeon more, moving outlying yellow flowers out of the way, she reached the edge and repositioned herself so her feet dangled over the rocky rim. She swiped gently across the tops of the wildflowers on her right and watched them spring back upright. Feeling reckless, she too swayed repeatedly, forward and back.

Wait for the watcher. The Father has yet a plan for you.

Although she had no idea what the statements meant, separate or together, she stopped wavering. Carefully she backed away from the bluff until she could come to a stand without risk of accidental suicide. "I'm sorry," she voiced to whoever this speaker was, "for being beastly a few minutes ago." Gazing around, expecting to see some specter or glowing light, she said no more in case the apparition spoke again.

For the next twenty minutes, it was quiet. All that could be heard was the sound of nature: the waves lapping and crashing on the shore below, the wind moving air and foliage at her feet, chirping and squawking of a myriad of birds. She closed her eyes and lay back. If she weren't so lonely, Ivers could be Heaven. Without Grey and her parents, it was definitely not even close.

Just a Dream

†

OR NEARLY A month longer, Mallory went about life pretending. She immersed herself in her work, the fight against genetic replication of Adam's DNA. All the while, she hoped that what the voice on the cliff top had said was true. Albeit the circumstances, she didn't view it as an unrealistic fantasy since the surreal visitor had reinforced Mrs. McKnight's premonition the day of Grey's burial. Yet, nothing came of either foretelling and Mallory's patience ran out and she began to revisit her plan to separate herself from her current and past life.

Preemptively, she mentioned to Paisley and Keaton a farfetched story about wanting to go off somewhere secluded to write her memoirs. Of course, Paisley was resistant, disbelieving her friend's desire to share with the world the privacy she insofar had guarded. This time, Mallory would be prepared; she knew she had to offer a convincing explanation. So not long after planting the seed, she presented Paisley with an outline of her life and what she wanted to pour into this book, stating the resulting biography wasn't so much for public consumption as it was for her own peace of mind.

She didn't need her friend's permission. Yet, if she could just leave knowing Paisley wasn't going to try to impose the life she thought Mallory should lead on her again, after two weeks or a month, she would feel much better. Although she was well beyond half-ways, she wanted to starve herself, to become a walking zombie if she felt like it. After her parents' death, in her aloneness, she had learned a good deal about herself. She had wished she'd had someone who loved her and only her in that unconditional way of parents. But that couldn't be, so she swallowed the reality of it. There were no grandparents or aunts and uncles who'd suddenly emerged from a long lost genealogical chart to claim her, welcome her with open arms, having known all about her without being told.

Odd as it may seem, she also wanted to give her love to someone, even though she was afraid of the same as well. Hesitant and skeptical as she might have been, when Grey came along he'd made all of her dreams *and fears* come true. She learned she'd wanted both because not only was perfection impossible it was unrealistic and boring. All in all, she came to realize upon his death that life without at least one consuming kind of relationship was meaningless; just a sequence of days strung together to pass the time.

She loved Paisley, but her best friend was moving in a direction with her life that included Mallory less and less every day, making her feel all the more childish when her friend doted on her as though she were simpleminded. Paisley and Everett would be married soon. They'd spoken of children, which meant the Brandts would be a family of their own someday. Mallory would be an aunt by association only. And Keaton … well, the situation there resolved itself too—after a poignant quarrel between them.

One evening several weeks ago, Mallory had gone without

sleep for over twenty-four hours again; her schedule had been completely thrown off since Grey's death, which she hadn't tried very hard to realign. Regardless, late that particular night Keaton came over for no apparent reason, bringing with him a bottle of very smooth, aged seventeen-year-old, Glenlivet Scotch. She woke up the next morning to find him sleeping beside her in her bed; although she didn't immediately realize it was Keaton's chest against which her back was snuggled. She'd turned around slowly, blissfully thinking Grey's death was just a horrific nightmare.

The shock she felt when facing her actual bedmate made her yell out in alarm, and still, the heart-wrenching cry did not wake Keaton. At first confused, she assessed the situation under the covers. She was wearing the same t-shirt and underwear as the day before, but she didn't recall having herself removed her sweater, bra, jeans, and socks when climbing into bed. Keaton was similarly undressed. At that point, using the full strength of her arms and legs, she shoved his bulky frame off the bed. He landed on the floor with a heavy thunk.

Upon this abrupt awakening, he grinned up at her stupidly, chuckled, and then joked how Mallory's passionate nature translated differently in the clear light of day. He also said something about regret, which seemed to imply further that what she feared happened, had, in fact, happened.

"Keaton, cut the cheek." Crouched on her knees, perched above him, she demanded he tell her the truth.

Finally, he confessed. What occurred the night before was she conked out after imbibing only one small glass of the potent malt whiskey. "You were knackered, Indy. Collywobbles and all, after jus' a wee dram of the finest." Then, he'd carried her into the bedroom and undressed her. Given the lateness, nearly two a.m., he let the temptation of her warm body tease him into committing a tiny violation of their friendship. He'd slid into the bed next to her—"Honest, my sweet," he promised—with the sole intention of sleeping. However, after the explanation of events, he went on to proposition her with a notion he thought was an inevitability, a relationship between them.

In dry humor, he said they could skip dating since now they'd already been to bed together, and besides that, had known one another practically their whole lives. He added that she couldn't mourn her student helper forever, emphasizing, "After all, Grey had been only a *boy*friend." Yet, Keaton knew, very well, that Mallory had planned to propose before the rude reality had shattered that idea.

It had been a mere few weeks, the pain of losing Grey was still so tender, even more so at that moment when the nightmare became real again. Her composure hung by a thread, constantly pulling at a sharp wound in the center of her chest. Thus, at that moment, it was Keaton's very offer that brought her serrated anger to the surface. As aforementioned, she wanted a *someone*, but that person was not Paisley's brother. She could not feel for him how he felt about her, nor how she felt about Grey. And that was putting it mildly.

She'd had enough of Keaton's obtuseness. She went ballistic; lecturing him first about the pointlessness of wishful thinking, then chastising him for disgustingly differentiating himself as a "man" and Grey a "boy," and finally progressing with her need to vent until she was calling him, "a manipulative, selfish, barmy creep" whose logic of inevitability was guided almost completely by the "unsatisfied, even repressively blue, knob between your legs." To punctuate her insults, she threw a few objects from the nightstand at him. A hard edge of the alarm clock nicked the wall just past his head.

Needless to say, he was stunned into speechlessness. He knew Mallory was forthright; and he'd seen her anger before, however, never had her fury been aimed at him. He left without preamble and avoided her for weeks afterward.

Mallory felt guilty for her tirade. It was mean; the last statement was in no way a fair assessment of Keaton's character, but she was relieved in finally having closed a door resolutely in his face. For a long time, she'd wanted him to come to the conclusion on his own—that in growing up together, despite one pubescent make-out session, they couldn't be anything to one another but friends.

Pinpointing the rationale of *why not* was impossible since ironically, she'd never thought of him as a sibling even though she'd thought of Paisley as a sister. Although she'd never admit it to either of them, Mallory had had a flaming crush on Keaton for two solid years beginning when she was fourteen; an infatuation that magically faded with a kiss, a gossamer-like moment of cognition, and the kiss giver's departure to college.

Back in the reality of adulthood, when she saw Keaton next, she brusquely apologized for her exaggerated response. He accepted the apology like the gentleman he was, but the rift that now existed between them was also plain to see on his face. During the seemingly normal conversation that followed, she noticed that he addressed her by her given name, which he rarely ever used. Gone was the nickname he'd bestowed on her at the age of thirteen.

Accidentally Dying

✝

T HROUGH HER OWN covert diligence, she finally found
the ideal spot—a rustic little cabin at the base of the
Colorado Mountains—where she could hide away
from civilization for a good long while. No one was likely to
drop by and she could wallow in her new-found addiction to
sleep. The longer she allowed herself to sleep, the longer she
wanted to. It dulled her senses; making the fewer waking hours
easier to bear. However, the solitude and the induced comatose
state she kept herself in these nearly two months took its toll in
other ways.

She'd taken to talking to herself. She was sane still, but
acutely aware that she was driving her mind to the very brink
of madness as well as her body to frailty by disuse or rather un-
use. Back at home, she hadn't slept at all for unnaturally long
spans of time. Now she slept the days away, waking up to get
some sustenance in her mouth, relieve nature calls, or go
through the motions of living until she could fall asleep again.
She had grown even thinner and weaker, for she nourished
herself too little, and it was not that she donned the same
clothes day in and out; she slept in them, lived in them for a
week at a time—like Grey's woolen sweater.

In this way, in a lonely, hand-hewn, log cabin in the
woods, Mallory managed to do exactly what she set out to

do—*nearly* self-destruct. For, she didn't have a foolproof strategy of how to actually kill herself; really, that wasn't the goal. She knew enough of the basics of Christianity to know life was considered a gift and ending that life, by a person's own hand was an unforgivable sin. Heaven was barred to sinners. At least, the information she'd found on the internet during her research told her so, and she needed to make it through those gates. Thus, for now, she only wanted to die on the inside … to live without the pain, to just stop *feeling* until true death came for her.

On one hand, by doing nothing—not participating in life—she was mocking that gift, yet on the other, by consciously not casting the blessing of life into the abyss herself, she was staving off Hell. She rationalized; it couldn't be so simple—to be condemned for loneliness—regardless that that solitude was self-imposed.

Even from the great distance of thousands of miles, her twisted methodology required effort. Since once a week, Paisley phoned mid-afternoon her time. Mallory would set an alarm clock to wake her up at six-thirty in the morning just for that call. This arrangement and time difference made it easy to explain the sometimes grogginess apparent in her voice. Furthermore, she refused to press "Connect" when the notification on her phone said there was an incoming video call. Paisley would board a plane within the hour if saw the sallowness of her best friend's skin, her cracked lips, and the stringy dirtiness of her hair.

Evoking energy she didn't feel, specifically for these status updates, Mallory spoke mainly of her memoirs project. It had actually turned out to be less fake an endeavor than she intended and Paisley learned more than she ever knew about her friend's turmoil.

"Do you remember when I broke my right arm and my dad turned his den into a schoolroom?"

"Yes. Nice of him to teach both of us the art of being ambidextrous."

"At the end of a month, I could hold a magnifying lens securely with my teeth so I could use my left hand to clean off the debris from our buried treasures."

"That's when my writing in all caps began."

"You still do. With both hands. Anyway, that story is in chapter three."

"What I don't remember is how you broke your arm in the first place."

"The actual event was unmemorable. Distracted, I tripped over a stone, fell forward awkwardly onto my wrist and my scrawny ulna snapped like a twig. Well, not really, but—"

"Your mom would give us long division problems."

Mallory chuckled. "As though a broken arm addled the brain. She was right to ask us to exercise the mind along with the hand. I can still write legibly with both left and right. At first, though, I don't know why but sixes were harder to write than nines; some percentage of the time, my nines *were* sixes. I got many answers wrong. Funny thing is I think I got better at maths afterward."

Although happy memories, Paisley could hear her friend sniffling into the phone, both during and a little after one of her reminiscences.

For Mallory, she'd initially used the memoirs excuse to escape her life, but when during her few cognizant hours each day she began to reminisce aloud, she soon found herself actively reflecting on the life that she thought she had wanted to forget. And writing her story through the eyes of misery in loss, she rediscovered this other purpose for her hermit-hood. She came to realize it the day she recalled her mother's gentle but effective way as she brushed out the tangles in her hair. To shed as much of her selfish grief as possible and remember her loved ones, surely as they wanted to be remembered, was the best tribute in the world to them as well as being a balm for Mallory's aches. It wasn't in pursuit of peace or even to relieve herself of the grief that she did this. In letting go, at least, the pain, she hoped instead to summon their virtual presence as though to keep her company (since no live person could fill the chasm her mother, father, and Grey had left in her chest).

Fireflies

†

ONE MONDAY, AFTER getting off the telephone with her only regular communicant, Mallory exited the cabin to get some fresh air into her lungs. Cautiously she made her way down to the pier, careful not to spill her coffee. As though twice her age, she descended sideways down the three steps before reaching the platform. A black and green rowboat sat docked to the side of the deck, bobbing ever so gently, inviting her to foray out even further, but Mallory didn't have the physical strength to navigate toward the serenity that the excursion might bring. A reassuring but morbid thought occurred to her while she pondered her laziness. *I would surely drown if I went for a swim.* Then she wondered if knowing this and deciding to do it anyway, would count as suicide. She harrumphed to herself and approached the furniture sprawled on the deck instead.

The mountains beyond reflected upon the glassy, black lake. Since she had grown content with her depression, she dismissed the beautiful sight sprawled before her as mundane when it was anything but ordinary. A sparkle on the surface of the water, from a ray of light peeking through a crevice between clouds, forced her to notice it. A warmth seemed to spread inside her, and for some unknown reason, she felt happier than she had in a long time.

Setting the brimming coffee cup on the small table, she lowered herself into the weathered Adirondack chair beside it. She pulled the sleeves of Grey's sweater over her fingers. Grasping the mug once again, she brought it to her nose, inhaling the aroma. The air outside was cool; the coffee would be temperate enough to drink shortly but she blew at the rim of the overly hot brew anyway. She held the warm, ceramic vessel as tightly as she could between both slippery sweater-covered hands while looking fixedly at the shimmering spot in the distance.

Feeling the growing desire to rejoin the world of the living, suddenly, Mallory decided it was time to go home. She wasn't accidentally dying and maintaining her current malaise was progressively getting more tiring. She was cognitive of the fact that she uncontrollably groaned like an old woman went she stood and again when she bent down. Getting through the perpetual stiffness in her limbs was beginning to wear on her nerves as moving seemed to require greater effort than she remembered exerting when her body was more conditioned to being active. Although these past couple of months were enlightening, she missed the *silent* fluidity of her movements, a regular day and night schedule, Paisley's and Keaton's spontaneous laughter, and even their sporadic company.

Of course, her chest still ached for Grey but it would seem she had to live out this life regardless. For the first time in many months, she smiled and just as she did, iridescent specs rose from the water like fireflies and floated toward her. She didn't know if it was a hallucination but she watched, mesmerized. The particles of light all stopped at the edge of the dock, continuing to merge toward one another until they formed themselves into a recognizable shape. After however long that took, an almost solid being hovered in front of her. Have I finally, completely lost it? she wondered.

The fantastical creature stood a dozen feet tall, clothed in a pearly white shroud seemingly made of cloth—the same color as the rest of him or *her*—and ethereal, massive, cloud-like wings stretched out behind it.

Mallory continued to stare, too stunned to do anything else. The appendages billowed forward in a flutter and then dropped, folding neatly at the figure's sides. Without taking her eyes from the scene, she groped for the surface of the small table so as to set her coffee down. Tentatively, she then reached out to touch the ghost. The apparition returned the gesture, yet she felt nothing tactile; the contact was more of a sensation, a familiar tingle.

"Grey?" she blurted without thinking, although this androgynous entity in no way looked like him.

No, Mallory. After a short pause it added, *We are but messengers.*

"Oh," she muttered in her stupefaction, cocking her head slightly to one side in order to glance at the periphery around the great specter. As far as she could see there were no others present. She returned her attention to the angel, staring into the colorless eyes that she would later imagine were greenish-gold even though those exact orbs did not belong to Grey.

Daughter, you were headed down the wrong path. We know you have taken the first step in correction.

"I was? I have?" She couldn't formulate complete

sentences. Aside from being distracted by the vision, her eyes were glued to the figure's expressionless face. It was speaking but *his* mouth wasn't moving. Yet, the voice emanating from those unspeaking lips was clear and seemed to drown away all other outside noise. The lapping water against the sides of the rowboat, the faint sounds coming from the surrounding trees, even her own breathing were no longer audible.

The Almighty can read your soul, along with it, your thoughts. You, yourself, are blind but soon you will see.

She couldn't know for sure if she was talking to a figment of her own imagination or some actual (albeit unreal) *thing*, whatever *it* was. "See what exactly?" she ventured again. That was probably not the most profound first question to pose to an apparently divine being. And although she was possibly, or should have been, honored by such a visit, she was human. Without some attempt at clarity, the experience would teeter on the verge of her sanity, a place where sleep and waking were interchanged, where one could believe lightening bugs were the substance of which angels were made. Still, humoring herself as it were, she'd been waiting ever since Mrs. McKnight uttered the possibility and had become even more expectant after that first voice came to her at the cliffs. Both conversations, if they could be called that, were vague. Thus, she was already full of notions and wanted what strange facts she could gather.

Patience is a virtue, the angel intoned softly.

"Mm. And if you knew I'd decided a correction of my *path* the moment I made that decision, then you would also know I've been forewarned before, forewarned and patient. Was it you who visited me before?"

Messengers function as one. That is all we can say to make you understand, however, understanding of our legion's ways is irrelevant. The tone in which this was spoken was matter-of-fact, if not kindly bland, but she was certain there was an implied "again" in the speech, as though the being was reminding itself of the value of patience.

Mallory, leave here, return to your rightful place as planned, and know this: humanity is at risk. Therefore, you must do what you can to warn others and await the watcher.

The last part still made no sense. Who was the watcher? How would she recognize him? For that matter, how was she meant to warn others? Did the spirit expect her, a sudden and unlikely devotee, to become a preacher?

You were his savior. If you do not recognize him, he will make himself known in some other way.

Had she saved Grey? She remembered him saying she would—save him. Flabbergasted at the idea, her mind glossed over the fact that the angel had answered questions she had not voiced. Why would she not recognize him? Her befuddled mind asked and dismissed quickly. For her heart reeled as it exalted too. She would see him again!

He may not come in the form you expect. If he does return to his human coil, it is possible you will not remember this conversation. Thus, and until then, attempt to prevent the resurrection of the Nephilim. That is the task requested of you—if only for the sake of your fellow humans. There may be little use, but try.

If the apparition were not so beautiful, he would be creepy. Even with her rudimentary knowledge of Heaven and its servants, she did not think they had the power to read her mind.

We cannot. However, as we said, the Father can. When our mission requires it, He provides the necessary gift or insight we do not inherently possess.

Homecoming

✝

A S SOON AS Mallory rounded the bend of the ramp off the airplane and glimpsed the sudden smiles of greeting as they turned placid in recognition, she knew. The day of homecoming wasn't going to be a pleasant one. Paisley and Keaton both stood with their legs slightly apart and arms crossed over their chests, gaping at her as she walked closer toward them through the exit corridor. When she was at last within speaking distance, Paisley grabbed hold of her upper arm, shook it, and squeezed the flesh, testing the extent of emaciation. What her friend found was disturbing. Under the fluffy padding of her down jacket, she was nothing but skin-covered bone.

Paisley looked to her brother with a deeply furrowed brow while Keaton shook his head in disbelief. His Indy had changed so dramatically since Grey's death. She had once been strong despite her petite stature. The woman standing before him looked smaller still and as frail as a dry leaf. Her rejection had been painful, but seeing her now broke his heart. Solemnly he asked if he should carry her to the car.

Sheepishly, Mallory smiled at Keaton and joked that she might take him up on the offer, knowing that a few months of mothering from her best friend were also to ensue. She'd had her bout of solitude and now she was ready to be revived, ready for the work that lay ahead. On the plane she'd decided, it was time Paisley was made aware of everything. She needed her friend for the mission. Therefore, agreeing without argument to return directly to Paisley's house, Mallory asked after Everett. Although the story needed to be told, no other person should be made privy to the mind-blowing knowledge.

As they all stood in front of the baggage carousel, although Mallory had been forewarned of the pending likelihood, it was then that Paisley announced her engagement to Everett had been finally made official. She went on to premise the plan with, "And Everett will be moving out of his small flat, selling his house in London … That means I'll be placing my house on the real estate market as well. He is in the midst of purchasing a grand manor, which is much more everything than we need but it's better situated in a number of ways, even if it isn't in Ivers proper. A few months from now we'll be settling into the house in Portreath."

Keaton didn't say much, but off and on, he continued to eye Mallory curiously as he retrieved her luggage and deposited it onto the floor beside him.

"In— Mallory, is that all?" he asked, looking down at the two small suitcases, both of which weighed nothing, as though empty.

Her eyes followed the rotation of the carousel, "That one's mine as well," she said, identifying a duffle bag just then coming through the plastic curtain at the top of the conveyor belt. While he walked around to collect the last bag, she took the opportunity to tell Paisley that a two-day, private, girl-bonding session was in order. There was much she wanted to tell her; many secrets she needed to reveal.

Keaton chauffeured the ladies to his sister's doorstep, carried the baggage into the foyer, but turned around and left immediately thereafter. During the time Mallory was away, he had tried to become accustomed to the idea of a dream lost, almost managing to convince himself as healed. Yet, setting eyes on her again only made him feel sick. More than ever, he wanted to be with her. The desire to wrap his arms around her and shield her from the world was too great a risk to take at the moment. She would surely shun him again. However, a tiny shred of hope existed still, that she would reconsider once she'd finished mourning the man who hadn't deserved her in the first place. As he climbed back in the car, he schooled himself in patience.

Story Time

†

P AISLEY'S HOUSE WAS gloomy; she seemed to prefer the dim, filtered light that came through curtains, whereas, Mallory preferred unadorned windows with views of sky and nature. Especially now, after living in a cabin, surrounded by woods for a long time—albeit amidst beautiful scenery—the bright light that *could* stream in through large windows was invigorating.

At the moment, they both sat in the center of Mallory's bed in the large spare room she'd stayed in before. The floor to ceiling drapes, which flanked the sliding glass doors in the room, were pulled as far back as they would go and tied into a knot. A tea cart laden with sandwiches, cookies, and tea, kept warm in a pot covered with a cozy, was pulled up beside them for snacking. Her hostess plied her with food at every moment and she did her best to eat. After taking a sip of tepid tea, she bit into a ham and Swiss cheese sandwich and chewed halfheartedly, considering where to begin. It was difficult to talk about Grey without feeling sad, but she had practiced feeling good, over bad.

"The day we weeded out the team … Blimey, that was over two years ago … anyway, Grey kissed me. Other people see fireworks or feel butterflies in their bellies, for me, my whole body hummed with a strange current."

"That's sweet," Paisley commented, looking at her friend sympathetically, thinking this conversation was another sort of grief therapy, and as though Mallory was an orphan reminiscing about rescuing an abandoned puppy.

"Paiz, I'm trying to tell you a story. And it's just the beginning so remove that 'Aw, you poor thing—the hardships you've gone through' expression from your face this instant. Besides, you're overdoing it. Be normal will you!"

Paisley smiled fondly at her spunky friend, glad to have her back. "Aye aye, Junior Peon."

"That's the spirit. I was saying, or thinking before I was going to say it … I can't believe I tried to shove my parents out of my head as if in not talking about them they could ever be forgotten. As though the pain of remembering them was worse than the joy of their memory."

"Aly, I'm sorry. I am. I thought I was helping by not bringing them up, but our weekly talks these past few months made it clear that's what you needed from me."

"I know." She accepted her best friend's apology because her time away had drawn this out also. She did blame Paisley to a degree—for not knowing what Mallory needed. She had needed an ally against the grief, not someone to help her erect an impenetrable wall.

There was a prolonged lull while Mallory recalled where she was in her story. "Well, I mentioned how I felt about that first kiss because I didn't realize until later that the feeling was odd in as much as it was special. For months, I knew very little of Grey. He was so secretive and I was inept, in general with relationships, as you well know. Finally, one day, when we were sitting in a sparse room on the second floor of his house and I was thinking I'd fallen for one weird bloke, perhaps with a shady side to him, I asked him to tell me about himself before I turned him into a full-fledged psycho in my head." She went on to recount the basic details of his family, stopping just before the big reveal.

"He grew up in a strange household, to say the least. Not abusive by any clear definition, but to me, his father repeatedly attacked him emotionally. In fact, for his entire life, beginning when he was just a young boy, he'd been brainwashed by heretics and as a result, Grey was a traumatised and tortured adult. He felt he bore the weight of the entire McKnight family on his shoulders. Now, before I tell you the next bit, you have to keep an open mind."

"All right," Paisley said skeptically.

Mallory took the single word as a promise and proceeded. "He showed me a birthmark, unlike any you, or I or anyone has ever seen. Almost his entire back was covered by this stain." Explaining this and not being able to show Paisley was harder than she thought it would be. Then an idea came to her that would illustrate the brand on Grey's back in a way that Paisley could visualize it herself. "The etching on the Gwellen henge stone and on Golly's, Adam's, and Tiny's temples was tattooed over Grey shoulder blades. A wing on either side of a human figure."

"Wait, you're saying he had a tattoo done to mask over his birthmark? Strange ... after we unearthed the stones ... stranger still. I can understand why you might have thought him dodgy."

"No, no. That was my confusion as well. I'm botching the explanation. It looked like a tattoo. I thought it was, but *that* was the birthmark. And not something vague you can interpret like a bunny in a cloud. It looked drawn on *like* a tattoo."

"Aly, no disrespect to the man you loved but Grey was obviously pulling the wool … rotten of him to ask you to believe it. He might as well have don a red suit. Maybe he *had* more in common with his manipulative family then you think. If he didn't know it, then he was certifiable."

She found Paisley's reaction ironically funny; she too had been cynical, recalling her accusation that Grey was part of some dark cult. "What did I say? Keep an open mind. Now, let me finish at least the start of it all so I can eventually get to the rest. This might take longer than a couple of days if you keep interrupting with half-boiled comments."

Going backward she explained Grey's upbringing in greater detail and then the history of the fallen angels as she'd been told. She reminded Paisley of India and Nigel as well as of the indisputable evidence that was the giants' carcasses. "Why do you suppose Grey, a semiologist, would submit a report of each aspect of a symbol in separate parts? He knew exactly what that emblem meant, as a whole. But in proclaiming that knowledge, he'd have to reinforce it somehow, without sensationalizing it like Nigel did. The problem was there was no way to prove it. The symbol cannot be found anywhere among human records. And so, is it any wonder the only explanations we've gotten so far make the etchings some tribal or ritualistic thing—done at birth on the malleable skulls of infants and on the stones upon death, like an epitaph? For that matter, has it never occurred you to wonder how wrong the scientific community is about the timeline of events?" Mallory nibbled her sandwich and sipped her tea while eyeing her quiet friend, whose facial expression was unreadable. She didn't want to rush through the story; as mentioned, Paisley must understand.

Paisley fell back in the bed and stared at the small chandelier that hung from the center of a plaster medallion in the ceiling. "My head is buzzing with questions about the Gwellen site, but I'm still having difficulty pinpointing what you're telling me about Grey. I know they are connected by the semiology, but how, exactly?" She rose to her elbows and looked at Mallory expectantly.

Paisley, too, wasn't religious, or rather, she was as complacent about religion as Mallory had been prior to being visited by two angels in the past few months. She still wouldn't dub herself a convert since she had always believed in God; that was never the question. She just hadn't made Him a fixture in her life. Like the majority of the human population she went about life trusting what she could see or decipher clearly with her senses but now, having seen a spiritual being, she was more cognizant, especially of a particular statement that that being had made: "You are blind but soon you will see."

Considering she had been prepared long before those visits—by Grey—the fact that Paisley couldn't comprehend the significance of the big picture was understandable. Also, her telling of the story was disjointed compared to how Grey had explained it. Thus, again, she tried to connect the pieces by first relaying Mrs. McKnight's words to her at the funeral, second repeating the history of the Nephilim, and finally including the vision Grey had had after India's and Nigel's fallen angel yarn went public.

Afterward, the two best friends sat quietly staring at each other; Paisley probably still in a state of confusion, trying to absorb everything and Mallory waiting to continue with the tale and the reason for divulging this all now.

Paisley slid off the bed. Standing next to the cart, she bent over, felt the outside of the teapot, and began to wheel the rickety contraption around the bed.

"We're not done you know?"

"Oh!" Paisley exclaimed, stopping in the doorway.

"Mm. I need two solid days of your attention, remember?"

Looking down at the picnic remains she said, "You've eaten approximately an eighth of your share of what is on this trolley. I promise to return and be attentive—although my head might explode—if you promise to stop consuming what amounts to crumbs."

Mallory chirped.

"I'll just make us a fresh pot but leave you with a question. Are you thinking we need to do anything now to set the record straight, about this fallen angel business?"

She opened her mouth to give a quick reply, but Paisley held up a hand, "Hold the thought; I'll be back before you know it."

Not even two minutes later Mallory heard Paisley's voice, presumably, she was on the phone. When next she heard Grey's name mentioned she rushed out of the room, waving frantically in front of her friend's face. "Paiz, what I've told you was private!" she huffed in an outraged whisper.

She scowled and shooed away her friend. "Yes, it's good to have her back. I'm trying to stuff my little chickadee with all kinds of goodies, but the scrawny thing is stubborn. I'll call you later. Mm-hm. Absolutely. Bye." As soon as she hung up the telephone, she pounced back with a reply. "Have you lost sight of the fact that I've known you for practically thirty years? I know the difference between a confidence and something I *would* share, even with Everett."

"How did Grey come up in the conversation then, eh?"

"I can't even mention his name? For your information, my exact phrase was, 'We are reminiscing about Grey, which is nice.' Besides, what you told me took hours; I couldn't manage to retell it in under five minutes."

Mallory smirked, bobbing her head at the poignancy of Paisley's comments. "True. You're forgiven."

"What?! Sometimes I forget, even at forty, you're stroppy and always will be." Paisley smiled fondly at her best friend. She was glad to know that despite Mallory's unhealthy appearance, underneath, she was the same vivacious person as before the ordeal.

"I am not. I'm *bracket*, mild-tempered, always nice, and not at all easily agitated, *close bracket* ... and 'always will be.' You, on the other hand, are blinkered if you think me otherwise." She added, "Humph" and stalked away. Once back in her room, she whined loudly, "By the way, I'm hungry, mum."

Collective Brawn

†

AFTER THE TWO days passed and Mallory had emptied all her secrets, metaphorically speaking, on the surface between them, they convened in Paisley's office to go over the current state of affairs concerning the cloning of the giants. Although Mallory's comprehension of that early morning visit from the angel glowed in her memory, it was not a clear vision. The apparition had said, in an oddly comforting way, that she should try; but, she could not help feeling the ominous portent of the preceding statement, *There may be little use.* Thus, *try* she would.

At this point, they decided to bring Keaton and Everett into the strategy session. As a team, they could better investigate why the giants' genetics were of such interest— Was giant humanoid DNA the surefire cure for cancer or something?—and advocate against the research and any upcoming bioengineering efforts. The two men were not informed of the basis for this mission: the backstory and the angel's missive along with it or even the mention of the Nephilim (as though the connection could ever be far from anyone's mind nowadays). These incidental spiritual details were not necessary for them all to agree: while genetic research alone was excusable, to a degree, and understandable even, the full-on replication of the giants' DNA was neither.

The first step was to gain a more thorough understanding but in conjunction, they had to formulate a plan of action to stop the progression. This too was a challenge; the bigger one.

In being uninvolved so long, Mallory feared she had singed the bridge with Sir Henry and while the others did their part, she set about taking steps to mend her relationship with the media mogul. It seemed their best chance. She called Sir Henry's office but a new secretary at the receiving end of the phone effectively blocked her from speaking with Sir Trenton directly. Ms. Bailey never even put through her calls to voicemail, and as Mallory received no reply back after several weeks, she assumed the secretary had been only pretending to jot down the messages she'd left. However, it was quite possible backing would need to be gotten through alternate channels, anyway. Sir Trenton had officially retired just over two months ago, although he was still acting as an advisor for his sons who now actually ran the family empire.

She then tried every phone number in her received calls list, hoping to get a direct line to his personal phone. When that too didn't work, she called the corporate office and made an appointment to meet with James, the eldest son. As a last ditch effort, she requested Sir Henry's presence at that conference. Ms. Bailey, who pretended not to recognize Mallory's voice every time she phoned—highly unlikely—intoned in her high-pitched, distant, librarian voice that she would relay the message. Mallory could only hope this time the secretary would act true to her word.

Within a following month, the team had collected all manner of useless information, for most of it was misleading and just plan hype. There were those looking to spin the conspiracy yarn (of course) and others who, for unknown reasons, pieced together a story in a moment of enlightenment as though they had been preachers in hibernation all along. "Our Lord has delivered unto me a message for the peoples of this Earth. Heed my warning and repent of your sins, now! Or face the judgment of the Almighty," one such self-proclaimed conduit stated repeatedly.

Weeding through the morass, finally they gathered information that Biolab was being funded by the United States government, certainly no surprise since large research projects were often funded by governments. By digging still deeper Keaton also discovered a vague reference to the stand-alone word, BRAWN. It was stamped in very small letters at the top and bottom of a scanned military document dated the same date as the genetic research proposal submitted to BIAI. Doing a broader search for just the word in databases—that, incidentally, Keaton did not have authorized access to— revealed a somewhat clearer picture.

Staying with this vein of the investigation, next, he collected as much information as possible on US military strategies and budgets, as well as, the conflicts in which its military were currently involved. The rationale for cloning giants did not jump out of the data but, at this point, it didn't take a politician or scientist to understand how these two fields coincided. "A battalion of twenty-foot tall Goliaths would make for powerful defense, as well as offense. For the country that could manage it, that is," Keaton summarized, as the others agreed silently.

Although they all knew it, it would seem Grey had been right. Rather than expending energy to find solutions for peace and well-being for all living creatures, there were those who would create life in order to torture it to death, to harm it, put it purposely in harm's way, or use it to control others' lives.

Mallory had always wondered why combat-to-the-death was necessary among members of the same species, for mankind specifically, an highly intelligent species. In her twenties, when she uncovered her first weapon, she felt shattered learning soon after that it was not a hunting tool she'd found. She couldn't comprehend the bloodlust in those who fought with other human beings for the sake of possessing lands that would not belong to them when they died naturally anyway. She was educated, so she knew people valued their heritage and their religious beliefs, as well as felt a camaraderie with their land's people and patriotism for their country. However, all humans were *their people* and surely to kill another of their kind was not godly.

This was another reason she didn't involve herself in the civic goings-on. Politics was a life and death game. Usually, it was everyone's but the politician's life at stake—the soldiers, mainly, and the bystanders, if need be. Peace was almost always framed as the desired result of bloodshed, but she saw it as contradictory to the definition of the passive word itself. She rather thought peace was rationalized with death. She felt sympathetic, all the more, toward those who offered their lives in trust, and hate for the men behind smiles or masks of solemnity who asked for that trust, took it freely but gave so little in return.

She and her father had had endless discussions on the topic. Although he proudly proclaimed his military status to his daughter, the fact was he had ventured into the field early in his life, at the time, thinking he was simply doing something good for his country. It wasn't long after that he witnessed the massacre of other soldiers—regardless of the side they were on—as well as innocents, and these traumatizing events changed his philosophy forever. The military way of life became more so his focus than his purpose in that he appreciated one thing, the discipline of soldiering. He kept the habits and tossed the rationale for the commanded and condoned acts of group violence out the proverbial window.

In those talks, he never tried to convince his daughter that war was purposeful in any way. Instead, they talked about history, why a certain battle had happened, and how it had culminated in the deaths it did. Then they'd deliberate over the real result in the surviving people's lives after minor skirmishes or major wars. Mallory Jacks senior was the greatest influence of her life. She credited him with the shaping of her pacifist mind.

Thus, she came to realize why the angels, or God, had chosen her for this mission and perhaps understood a little of why she and Grey were soulmates. It was through this grand connection to the Nephilim. Grey was special. And non-pious as she was, she was special as well.

A Weakened State

S IR HENRY'S SUPPORT had been dependable (and powerful) at one time. Now, the distinct feeling of inevitability in losing their advantage with the most credible of scientific publishers was a one she could not shake. Her one and only meeting with James Trenton, Sir Henry's successor, had not gone promisingly. Still, in this meeting, they'd been granted another chance—which might very well be their last—given that at the very onset Mr. Trenton had assessed her from head to toe, curled his lip in premature decision, and remarked shortly that he only had ten minutes he could spare her.

Going in, despite this condescension, she was confident—recalling Sir Henry's self-righteous air, too, at their first meeting—for she'd had two would-be points going for her: James had read her previous articles and was at least informed on the subject matter and the secondly, Sir Henry's presence at the conference. Although, it did not take long for Mallory to realize these advantages were merely facts; neither point particularly in her favor.

Primarily, during her concise speech she tried to judge James's reception to her argument. She used the directness that was her way. But afterward, she was left with the impression that not only wasn't he convinced genetic cloning was an altogether bad idea, she had managed to personally raise James's hackles somehow.

As for still having a possible ally in Sir Henry, she had also once or twice looked to him and found there, little evidence of remaining support, at least none was apparent until very nearly the end of her pitch anyway. It was in this final uncomfortably silent moment that Sir Henry declared flatly—as though it was always a given—that Trenton Media would continue to publish anything she deemed worthy of printing. Unfortunately, as he had demoted himself to the role of mere advisor now, and perhaps he was still unused to his decisions being questioned, the small victory was short lived. James immediately denied the surety of his father's promise. Mallory fumed privately while waiting patiently to be told that the meeting had come to an end or for a glimmer of a sign the battle of power between father and son had yet to unfold. She was rewarded with a favorable outcome, although the small win was not fulfilling. For, in his astute way, Sir Henry handled the situation in way entirely too professional for Mallory's liking.

He stated, "James, any serious media resource must always present as many sides of a debate as possible, regardless of how adamantly he believes in one particular, opposing viewpoint. Otherwise, you risk from the onset the reputation of being perceived as biased, taking Trenton Media in a decisive direction. You see?"

James squared his jaw in defiance and briefly narrowed his eyes in displeasure but conceded to accept one article, claiming with a quick sardonic grin, "His people" would reevaluate her contributions after that.

Were it not for her respect for the wise old gentleman, Mallory would have told the upstart to pack his hand-me-down influence in a suitcase and carry it with him straight to Hell. In hindsight, she felt she should have done anyway; Sir Henry would have likely appreciated the scene.

That James, an identical, younger version was not going to be like his father in philosophical approach was a tad discouraging. But, only recently had she, Paisley, Everett, and Keaton made the connection with the military purpose for the giants and they were thankful that this secret once revealed would, at least, get the widest exposure now. Thus, she rushed to finish her first substantial article after her extended sabbatical, the one chance they had to present the other side to the world. As a later fallback, LEMM would publish her words. But, they all knew it would be a rather pointless effort; LEMM's reach, by comparison, was negligible—their voice would be that of a small band of rebels in the periphery screaming to be heard.

As she sat down at the kitchen table and reread her published argument in the *Anthroscience Journal*, Mallory noticed a new disclaimer: "The information supplied in this article may contain opinions not shared by its publisher." As the publication did not accept editorials and commentaries, per se, but rather thoroughly researched, informative articles, she was annoyed by this statement's implication. "Oh! How I wish I had told him to sod off." She pointed at the sentence when Paisley and Everett came up behind her.

"By Jove, that was rude of them to print."

"Readers of the *Journal* know better. It's not as though

you're an unknown nobody," Paisley said consolingly. However, she sounded less sure.

Hopefully, it was just a new policy. Mallory flipped the pages of the magazine, looking at the bottom of all the other articles for a similar statement. She slapped the cover shut and shoved the booklet away. At that moment, her phone vibrated and shimmied closer to the edge of the table. She steadied it with a finger and leaned over slightly to look at the caller ID. "Unknown." Suspecting Sir Trenton, she hurriedly fumbled to pick up the phone.

"Hello?"

"My son is inexperienced," the raspy voice said. "However, rest assured, my girl; he has heard from me, likely before you even saw the amateur's note in fine print."

"Yes, but that won't take it back!"

"I understand. Even printing a retraction in the next edition will do nothing but draw attention to it again." He paused. "I trust what you say is true, this most distressing news of what the Americans are planning. You stated the human genome is complex, but also that they've recently attained a major success. Have you any idea on when the world can expect a living prototype?"

"I haven't been able to get through to a geneticist specifically at Biolab who will talk to me. In speaking to another biologist, I learned an engineered-double does not need to age like a normal human, which is the scary part. In other words, once they've figured out enough of the code, they can replicate Adam within a matter of months exactly as he would have appeared the day he died. Let me repeat. They won't need the complete genome to bring him to life. Furthermore, the twin's mind will be a blank slate, trainable with whatever nonsense they teach him." The tone of her voice wavered.

"I have always tried to imagine the worst of consequences when deciding whether to support or reject a proposed advancement and I find this notion of Frankenstein soldiers horrendous. However, my opinions differ from my son's and the empire I have built is no longer within my direct control."

"What you're saying is he's going to make our goal harder to attain."

"Unfortunately, yes, it would seem so. In one respect, contrary to what you might think, James found your article revolutionary. He is even now taking measures to position Trenton Media amidst this globally impactful technology, strategising ways of being a key player in *support* of it. In light of this, although it is inconceivable to have reached this point, I fear we are too late, my dear."

"That may be but with all the pluses on their side there is one big minus that remains," she said solemnly.

"Which is?"

"They may be able to make him live but Adam 2.0 may not survive. It's a shame to think it, of a living creature I feel, but history has shown clones tend to live very short lives. For all our technological advancements, we're not at a stage to change that outcome yet."

"Can you think of no more we can do?"

"The fact is, Sir Henry, I'm an anthropologist, my friends are as un-influential as me and as you said, you're a *retired* businessman. None of us has the power; somehow, we have to reach someone who does. So, to answer your question, unless we can devise a way to stop the progress … perhaps by some legal avenue, then no."

"Dr. Jacks, Mallory, it is not like you to sound so pessimistic," Sir Trenton reprimanded, turning around on his own earlier defeatist statements. "That said, I chastise you as well as myself. You are not without your abilities and old as I am, I am not completely useless as of yet."

She nodded, as though he could see her when what was she was doing was agreeing with Sir Trenton's statement, trying to believe it. The moment she got off the phone, she let out an exasperated sigh. "Paiz, it's all my fault!"

"Don't you dare blame yourself for the greedy, misguided actions of others."

"Had I not gone barmy, had I taken Nigel's crappy poster seriously even a year ago, we might have severed the head of the dragon off at the neck."

Life Is for the Living

†

THE SUNSHINE SHONE brightly and the haze hugged the cliff's edge as the fog had done many times before. Although she tried to release herself, Keaton clasped her hand tightly in his; the wind might lift her up and carry her away. He had coaxed her into this walk because, despite her natural honey complexion, she still spent too much time indoors and the healthful color had yet to fully to her appearance.

"Paisley's mothering seems to have waned. Or she's given up," he said, pulling her closer to his side, grasping her elbow as well.

"Keaton! Cut it out. I'm not going to fall."

"Mm. Yes, but you're also a wisp."

"No more than ever. I've gained weight."

"You're still smaller somehow." It was true. Her personality had always made her seem larger than life and it was obvious, some of the spunk had diminished.

"What do you mean?" she asked abstractly, squinting at the horizon.

"Maybe you can't see it looking in the mirror … I don't know how else to say it … I know Paisley agrees with me. We've lost a part of you. *You* have lost a part of you."

"Mm-hm."

"Is it too much to hope for to have the old Mallory back someday? My Indy?"

"I lost my parents. Then Grey." She stopped, as though grief was an excuse that would last for the rest of her life.

"I'm not saying it won't always hurt, but it's been a little over four years since their death and several months since his and yet, you have to go on living."

"Tell me something I don't know."

"I'm your friend, you know that. For always. But despite what you think of what I'm about to say, I'm not guided by the 'knob between my legs.' That said, I'd like for you to think about life *with me* instead of, well, instead of miring yourself in the throes of death with him."

Slowly, she turned away from the ocean to face him. "Let's just see if there's anything to that then, shall we?" Standing in front of him, she rose on her toes and stiffly slipped her arms around his neck. Entangling her fingers through his thick black hair, she pulled his head down toward hers. Of course, he did not resist. The kiss was short and pleasant enough. As they stepped away from one another, she looked down blankly at the front of his shirt while he gazed upon her with a tiny grin. He held her petite hand in his and caressed the base of her thumb with repetitive back and forth strokes.

In her mind, the situation was far from romantic. She was well aware that everything he'd said was true; Keaton wasn't to know that she'd set all her hopes on Grey's return. She imagined that she would be herself again someday. And yet, the angel had told her, *He may not come in the form you expect.* Therefore, it was possible she might not ever know him again, as a woman knows a man. What if Grey came back as talking dust, like the messenger, an angel? Now that she was not waiting to die, could she go through the rest of her life without human touch—a man's embrace?

It was a risky game to play with Keaton, in particular. On the other hand, apart from picking up your random drunken playboy, just to appease her cravings for male attention from time to time, there was no other person with whom she could take that risk.

"Indy? Just so I'm clear—"

"Can we not make a case of it and just see how it goes?"

"That's all I needed to hear," he said softly, gazing at her for a moment longer. "Now, why don't we venture closer to the beach?"

The climb down the narrow path was steep. She skipped almost sideways—close against the rock face of the bluff—looking vibrant and alive to Keaton who followed close behind. When their feet were planted on the flat, rocky soil of the beach, she laughed, the exhilaration apparent in her cheeks.

"I think it is fair to suggest we make a habit of this," Keaton said, his own spirits buoyed.

She froze, the smile disappearing her lips. Having finally acknowledged his feelings after all this time, having accepted him as more than Paisley's brother and just a friend, suddenly Mallory felt burdened by his affection.

"What? What did I say?"

"Ehm, nothing. I was just thinking of Paisley."

"And why would thoughts of my sister sober your mood when you were blatantly enjoying yourself a moment ago? will

I reprimand her for being more matronly than motherly?"

"She might not understand," she ventured. The fact was— even though hers and Keaton's brand-new *involvement* hadn't yet gone beyond a kiss—she would have to explain herself to Paisley and was not looking forward to that confrontation. Paisley knew very well that Mallory was besotted with her dead almost-fiancée, and was still hopeful of being reunited with him.

"Don't worry about it. I happen to know a detail or two about Paisley. She'll be thrilled you and I are on the same page finally."

"Mm. Page one maybe … of different chapters."

"You speak in riddles, Indy."

The beach was strewn with smooth, round stones. She kicked one near her foot and watched it fly for a second before it landed with a sharp *clack* next to another. "Keaton, you should know, I'll always love Grey," she said evenly, having no problem saying it now. She could scream it from the highest ground.

He opened his mouth to speak, but instead bent down, picked up a rock, and hurled it precisely at the one she had relocated. His stone jarred the other out of place, nestling close to the one that remained relatively unmoved from before.

Mallory quietly walked over, re-situated the displaced stone in a circle with the other two, and then took her time separating all of them equidistantly one inch from each other. She turned around, placed her hands on her hips, and glared at Keaton, who shook his head and stared up at the clouds.

A little over an hour later, when they walked through the

door holding hands—which Mallory had insisted upon as a way of demonstrating their understanding outright—Paisley stomped toward them and hauled her friend into a room, slamming the door resolutely behind them.

The men likely heard a muffled argument, which began with: "Not that I wouldn't be happy if ..." Paisley's voice trailed away, only to elevate again. "If I thought you were ... my brother ... for Heaven's sake. Aly! You told me ... He doesn't know ... Grey."

In between, Mallory spoke but she was doing a better job of suppressing the pitches of an emotional rebuttal. After twenty minutes, both of their voices had lowered to a whisper and it was then when the ladies emerged from the room, both apparently still upset and reserved toward one another. Immediately, Paisley came to stand next to her brother.

A grinning Everett intoned, "Tsk, tsk," in Mallory's direction. To which, she raised her eyebrows and shrugged. She wondered what they'd heard but since Keaton, as well, was mildly amused, it couldn't have been anything he found too alarming. Not much that made sense, anyway.

The Ending

†

REGARDLESS OF POSSIBLY making a big mistake in re-stoking the fire of her teenage crush, every night Mallory prayed through a pinhole of hope, asking the watcher to hurry on his way. Grey had said his death would bring the Rapture and yet if that was so, why would he need to return? The question plagued her. She couldn't begin to fathom how her quest now was linked to Grey. She only knew she needed him. Bugger, the Rapture, she thought, I still want him to come back to me.

Meanwhile, the team fruitlessly continued to investigate and finagle every avenue available to them. Sir Trenton had laid at their disposal the best lawyers and advisors to guide their strategy but after several months they could still do nothing to stop the progression of the opposition. The fact was, thus far, Mallory and the rest had not succeeded in even delaying Biolab from making strides. Due in a large part to Trenton Media's clout—albeit a reputation not of Sir Henry's successor's making—, under James Trenton's management, Biolab had been granted more and more leeway. Open doors and greater funding meant growing efforts toward the desired outcome.

From the beginning of mess, rather than posing a new challenge, the leak of the United States' military plans in the United Kingdom *accomplished* three things for each country's government. It was with the support of biased news coverage that an agreement was formed between the nations: Adam, Goliath, and Tiny were to be loaned to the research facility and its laboratory in exchange for open communications on the development of viable results. Secondly, as the two nations were allies already, the UK would collaborate with the Americans to expedite research and development of a prototype. Finally, once clones were created, an unprecedented treaty would be established.

Furthermore, on March 30, 2019, little more than a year from when Nigel's revelation first appeared in *The Endish Daily* and less than a year since the bio-research debate started the Prime Minister, Geoffrey Kincaid, announced that within the next ten years the US President would be made Chief Commander of both countries' military efforts.

That these countries' leaders anticipated an entire citizen-less army to be created in such a relatively short period of time was mind-boggling until Mallory and the others learned another shocking fact. A robotics company would be integrating cybernetic armors and components into the new soldiers, which would reinforce the bioengineering and thus, eliminate the biggest setback—the longevity of the life of clones.

At this point, Mallory and her team knew their cause was truly lost. As if on cue, the same evening as the latest discovery, she was finally, and once again, visited by a spirit messenger, who confirmed the absolute defeat.

Having let the scenario play out, the Heavenly Estate was now certain of the human world's future—without God's intervention. The messenger was clear, in a way that only a fantasy vision can be, and still, Mallory did not fully comprehend what she was being told. She surmised the broad facts. Civilization would perish in a world war and the spirits of the Nephilim in the other world would embody man-made soldiers. They would then occupy the planet as their new dominion. Humans that remained would be slaves to underworld masters.

She asked after Grey and was informed.

It was for the goodness of Noah that God wanted the Earth be cleansed again of the corruption that stained it, the land of His second children. Yet, even after the Great Flood the darkness persisted. It grew. It is now in the soil, the air, the water, and the souls of the forever tainted. And thus, Mallory, the time of the watcher is necessarily close at hand. A cleanse is coming and regardless of what is written in your numerous texts, Heaven shall not be on Earth.

The End

About the Author

Ellison Blackburn lives with some of her favorite beings in beautiful, high-tech Seattle, Washington.

An early interest in the soft sciences, together with a career in information technology, ignited Ellison's curiosity in singularities many years ago. Most intriguing is the constant line-toeing taking place between humanity and advancement, between who we are and what we will do in the name of progress. Thus, Ellison pens fiction that seems to crash like a wave over individual lives but rather leave a wake across societies too, stories that present multiple speculative ideas at once—because in real life, singularities will not manifest one after another in an orderly fashion.

Among her published works are *Flash Back*, book one of the women's speculative fiction Fountain trilogy; *If There Be Giants*, book one of science fiction and speculative fiction Watchers duology; *An Untimely End*, book one of the science fiction and historical mystery series, the Windy City Files; and the cyberpunk dystopian fiction novella *Virtue Us*, the Future of Love.

Titles by Ellison Blackburn

The Watchers

If There Be Giants
Second Son

The Windy City Files

From Time to Time [short story]
An Untimely End
No Time Like the Present

The Fountain

Flash Back
Second Nature
Being Human

The Future of Love

Tantamount [short story edition]
Virtue Us [novella edition]

Ebook and paperback editions of Ellison Blackburn's novels are available for purchase at major online book retailers.

Printed in Great Britain
by Amazon